PETER PAN

PETER PAN

J. M. BARRIE

Abridged by Neil Grant
Illustrated by Georgina Hargreaves

DEAN

Do you know that this book is part of the J.M. Barrie 'Peter Pan Bequest'?
This means that J.M. Barrie's royalty on this book
goes to help the doctors and nurses to cure the children
who are lying ill in the Great Ormond Street Hospital for Sick Children
in London.

This edition first published in 1985 by Dean, part of Reed International Books Ltd.,
Michelin House, 81 Fulham Road,
London SW3 6RB

Reprinted 1991

Copyright © abridged text Deans International Publishing
a division of The Hamlyn Publishing Group Limited 1985
Copyright © illustrations Deans International Publishing
a division of The Hamlyn Publishing Group Limited 1985

ISBN 0 603 00413 X

Produced by Mandarin Offset

Printed in Hong Kong

Contents

Introduction   10

Peter Breaks Through   12

The Shadow   16

Come Away, Come Away!   21

The Flight   30

The Island Come True   37

The Little House   45

The Home Under the Ground   50

The Mermaids' Lagoon   53

The Happy Home   63

Wendy's Story   68

The Children Are Carried Off   76

Do You Believe in Fairies?   79

The Pirate Ship   87

'Hook or Me!'   94

The Return Home   107

When Wendy Grew Up   116

Introduction

THERE ARE some fairy stories which everyone knows. You can no more grow up without hearing about Cinderella or Sleeping Beauty than you can without discovering that fire is hot and ice is cold. Most of these famous stories were not written by one person, certainly not by anyone we can name. They were first told hundreds of years ago, and passed down from parents to children, to the children's children, and so on. By the time someone thought of printing them in a book they were already ancient.

But there are a few – very few – fairy stories which were written in quite recent times, and yet have joined that sparkling band of children's favourites. *Peter Pan* is one of these.

The story of Peter Pan, the boy who would not grow up, was first published in 1911, three-quarters of a century ago. It was written by James Matthew Barrie.

Barrie was the ninth of ten children of a poor Scottish weaver, but by this time he was over fifty and a well-known writer of adult stories and plays. He had no children of his own, but he had grown very close to a family of five boys named Llewellyn Davies (he became their guardian after their father died). He used to make up stories to tell them, and Peter Pan started life in that way.

Peter Pan made his first public appearance in a book in *The Little White Bird*, an adult novel published in 1902. The full story came in the form of a play, called *Peter Pan*, which was first produced at Christmas time in 1904. Years later, Barrie said he couldn't remember writing it, but perhaps he was pretending; it was not always easy to tell with him. Although he was nervous about having the play performed, it was a terrific success, and it has been put on in London every Christmas ever since, except for one year (1940 – the most desperate year of the Second World War).

The final version of the story, the novel, is longer than the play, but the characters are the same and so are most of the amazing happenings.

J. M. Barrie liked children better than grown-ups, and he liked childhood better than adulthood. That is perhaps a sad thing for someone who is grown-up himself, but it helps to explain the success of *Peter Pan*. There is no story like this mixture of excitement and humour, of fantastic happenings and solid common sense. Probably no one except Barrie could have written a story which contains lots of violence and ferocity but is not at all nasty or frightening.

Some people are surprised that such a very 'English' hero as Peter Pan was invented by a man who never lived in England until he was grown up. But I think you might guess the author was a Scot. Peter has a canny shrewdness combined with a ready acceptance of make-believe that puts me in mind of one or two old Highlanders I have met.

This book is the story of Peter Pan as Barrie told it in its final form, but a little shorter. There are some parts which can be left out without spoiling the story. I have also added a few lines here and there and changed one or two words or phrases which would not be so easily understood today.

But this is a story about children quite a long time ago, and it would be silly to change things just to make them seem more like children today. This is Barrie's Peter Pan and Barrie's Wendy. Even if I wanted to, I wouldn't dare change them. I don't want that ticking crocodile coming after me.

Neil Grant

Peter Breaks Through

ALL CHILDREN, except one, grow up. They soon know that they will grow up, and the way Wendy knew was this. One day when she was two years old she was playing in a garden, and she plucked another flower and ran with it to her mother. I suppose she must have looked rather delightful, for Mrs Darling put her hand to her heart and cried, 'Oh, why can't you remain like this for ever!' This was all that passed between them on the subject, but henceforth Wendy knew that she must grow up. You always know after you are two. Two is the beginning of the end.

Wendy was the oldest. Then came John, then Michael.

For a week or two after Wendy came it was doubtful whether they would be able to keep her, as she was another mouth to feed. Mr Darling was frightfully proud of her, but he was very honourable, and he sat on the edge of Mrs Darling's bed, holding her hand and calculating expenses.

'I have one pound seventeen here, and two and six at the office; I can cut off my coffee at the office, say ten shillings, making two nine and six, with your eighteen and three makes three seven nine . . .'

There was the same excitement over John, and Michael had even a narrower squeak; but both were kept, and soon you might have seen the three of them going in a row to Miss Fulsom's Kindergarten school, accompanied by their nanny.

Mrs Darling loved to have everything just so, and Mr Darling had a passion for being exactly like his neighbours; so, of course, they had a nanny. As they were poor, this nanny was a prim Newfoundland dog, called Nana.

She was quite a treasure of a nanny. How thorough she was at bath-time; and up at any moment of the night if one of her charges made the slightest cry. Of course her kennel was in the nursery.

It was a lesson in propriety to see her escorting the children to school, walking sedately by their side when they were well behaved, and butting them back into line if they strayed. On John's football days she never once forgot his sweater, and she usually carried an umbrella in her mouth in case of rain.

No nursery could possibly have been conducted more correctly, and Mr Darling knew it, yet he sometimes wondered whether the neighbours talked.

He had his position in the city to consider.

Nana also troubled him in another way. He had sometimes a feeling that she did not admire him. 'I know she admires you tremendously, George,' Mrs Darling would assure him, and then she would sign to the children to be specially nice to father.

There never was a simpler, happier family until the coming of Peter Pan.

Mrs Darling first heard of Peter Pan and the Never Land when she was putting the children to sleep. Of course, their Never Lands varied a good deal. John's, for instance, had a lagoon with flamingoes flying over it, while Michael, who was very small, had a flamingo with lagoons flying over it. John lived in a boat turned upside down on the sands, Michael in a wigwam, Wendy in a house of leaves deftly sewn together.

But on the whole the Never Lands had a family resemblance.

Of all delectable islands the Never Land is the snuggest and most compact; not large and sprawly, with tedious distances between one adventure and another, but nicely crammed. When you play at it by day with the chairs and tablecloth, it is not in the least alarming, but in the two minutes before you go to sleep it becomes very nearly real. That is why there are night-lights.

Occasionally in her travels through her children's Never Lands Mrs Darling found things she could not understand, and of these quite the most perplexing was the word Peter. She knew of no Peter, and yet here he was in John and Michael's minds, while Wendy's began to be scrawled all over with him. The name stood out in bolder letters than any of the other words, and as Mrs Darling gazed she felt that it had an oddly cocky appearance.

'Yes, he is rather cocky,' Wendy admitted to her mother with regret.

'But who is he, my pet?'

'He is Peter Pan, you know, mother.'

At first Mrs Darling did not know, but after thinking back into her childhood she just remembered a Peter Pan who was said to live with the fairies. There were odd stories about him; as that when children died he went part of the way with them, so that they should not be frightened. She had believed in him at the time, but now that she was married and full of sense she quite doubted whether there was any such person.

'Besides,' she said to Wendy, 'he would be grown up by this time.'

'Oh no, he isn't grown up,' Wendy assured her confidently, 'and he is just my size.'

Mrs Darling consulted Mr Darling, but he smiled pooh-pooh. 'Mark my words,' he said, 'it is some nonsense Nana has been putting into their heads; just the sort of idea a dog would have. Leave it alone, and it will blow over.'

But it would not blow over; and soon the troublesome boy gave Mrs Darling quite a shock.

Some leaves of a tree had been found on the nursery floor, which certainly were not there when the children went to bed, and Mrs Darling was puzzling over them when Wendy said with a tolerant smile:

'I do believe it is that Peter again!'

'Whatever do you mean, Wendy?'

'It is so naughty of him not to wipe his feet,' Wendy said, sighing. She was a tidy child.

She explained that she thought Peter sometimes came to the nursery in the night and sat on the foot of her bed and played on his pipes to her. Unfortunately she never woke, so she didn't know how she knew, she just knew.

'What nonsense you talk, precious. No one can get into the house without knocking.'

'I think he comes in by the window,' she said.

'My love, it is three floors up.'

'Were not the leaves at the foot of the window, mother?'

It was quite true. The leaves had been found very near the window.

Mrs Darling did not know what to think. 'Why did you not tell me of this before?' she asked.

'I forgot,' said Wendy lightly. She was in a hurry to get her breakfast.

Surely, she must have been dreaming.

But, on the other hand, there were the leaves. Mrs Darling examined them carefully; she was sure they did not come from any tree that grew in England. She crawled about on the floor, peering for marks of a strange foot. She rattled the poker up the chimney and tapped the walls. She let down a tape from the window to the pavement, and it was a sheer drop of thirty feet, without so much as a spout to climb up by.

Certainly Wendy had been dreaming.

But Wendy had not been dreaming, as the very next night showed, the night on which the extraordinary adventures of these children may be said to have begun.

All the children were once more in bed. Mrs Darling had bathed and sung to them till one by one they had let go her hand and slid away into the land of sleep.

All were looking so safe and cosy that she smiled at her fears now and sat down tranquilly by the fire to sew.

The fire was warm, however, and the room dimly lit by three night-lights, and presently Mrs Darling was asleep.

While she slept she had a dream. She dreamt that the Never Land had come too near and that a strange boy had broken through from it.

The dream itself would have been a trifle, but while she was dreaming the window blew open and a boy did drop to the floor. He was accompanied by a strange light, no bigger than your fist, which darted about the room like a living thing.

Mrs Darling started up with a cry, and saw the boy, and somehow she knew at once that he was Peter Pan. He was a lovely boy, dressed in leaves, and the most entrancing thing about him was that he had all his first teeth. When he saw that she was a grown-up, he gnashed the little pearls at her.

The Shadow

MRS DARLING SCREAMED, and, as if in answer to a bell, the door opened and Nana entered. She growled and sprang at the boy, who leapt lightly through the window. Again Mrs Darling screamed, for she thought he was killed, and she ran down into the street to look for his little body, but it was not there.

She returned to the children's room and found Nana with something in her mouth, which proved to be the boy's shadow. As he leapt at the window Nana had closed it quickly, too late to catch him, but his shadow had not had time to get out. Slam went the window and snapped it off.

Nana hung the shadow out at the window, meaning, 'He is sure to come back for it; let us put it where he can get it easily without disturbing the children.'

But unfortunately Mrs Darling could not leave it hanging out at the window; it looked so like dirty washing and lowered the whole tone of the house. She thought of showing it to Mr Darling, but she knew exactly what he would say: 'It all comes of having a dog for a nanny.'

She decided to roll the shadow up and put it away carefully in a drawer, until a fitting opportunity came for telling her husband.

The opportunity came a week later, on that never-to-be-forgotten Friday. Of course it was a Friday.

'I ought to have been specially careful on a Friday,' she used to say afterwards.

'No, no,' Mr Darling always said, 'I am responsible for it all.'

They sat night after night recalling that fatal Friday. 'If only I had not accepted that invitation to dine at No. 27,' Mrs Darling said.

'If only I had not poured my medicine into Nana's bowl,' said Mr Darling.

'If only I had pretended to like the medicine,' was what Nana's wet eyes said.

They would sit there in the empty nursery, recalling every smallest detail of that dreadful evening. It had begun so uneventfully, so precisely like a hundred other evenings, with Nana carrying Michael on her back to his bath.

'I won't go to bed,' he had shouted, 'I won't, I won't. Nana, it isn't six o'clock yet. I won't be bathed, I won't, I won't!'

Mrs Darling had come in, wearing her white evening gown because she and

Mr Darling were going out to dinner. She soon quietened Michael.

Her two older children were playing at being herself and father on the occasion of Wendy's birth, and John was saying: 'I am happy to inform you, Mrs Darling, that you are now a mother,' in such a tone as Mr Darling himself may have used on the real occasion.

Wendy had danced with joy, just as the real Mrs Darling must have done.

Mr Darling too had been dressing for the party, and all had gone well with him until he came to his bow-tie. He came rushing into the children's room with the crumpled little brute of a tie in his hand, yelling: 'This tie, it will not tie.' He became dangerously sarcastic. 'Not round my neck! Round the bedpost! Oh yes, twenty times have I made it up round the bedpost, but round my neck, no! Oh dear no!'

Mrs Darling remained placid. 'Let me try, dear,' she said, and indeed that was what he had come to ask her to do. She tied his tie for him, Mr Darling forgot his rage, and in another moment was dancing round the room with Michael on his back.

The romp had ended with the appearance of Nana, and most unluckily Mr Darling collided against her, covering his trousers with hairs. Of course, Mrs Darling brushed him, but he began to talk again about it being a mistake to have a dog for a nanny.

'George, Nana is a treasure.'

'No doubt, but I have an uneasy feeling at times that she looks upon the children as puppies.'

'Oh no, dear one, I feel sure she knows they have souls.'

'I wonder,' Mr Darling said thoughtfully, 'I wonder.'

It was an opportunity for telling him about the boy. At first he pooh-poohed the story, but he became thoughtful when she showed him the shadow.

'It is nobody I know,' he said, examining it carefully, 'but he does look a scoundrel.'

Before he could say any more, Nana came in with Michael's medicine. Now, if Mr Darling had a weakness, it was for thinking that all his life he had taken medicine boldly. So now, when Michael dodged the spoon in Nana's mouth, he said reprovingly, 'Be a man, Michael.'

'Won't, won't,' Michael cried naughtily. Mrs Darling left the room to get a chocolate for him, and Mr Darling thought this showed want of firmness.

'Michael, when I was your age I took medicine without a murmur.' He really thought this was true, and Wendy, who was now in her night-gown, believed it also, and she said, to encourage Michael, 'That medicine you sometimes take, father, is much nastier, isn't it?'

'Ever so much nastier,' Mr Darling said bravely, 'and I would take it now as an example to you, Michael, if I hadn't lost the bottle.'

'I know where it is, father,' Wendy cried, always glad to be of service. 'I'll bring it,' and she was off before he could stop her. Immediately his spirits sank in the strangest way.

'John,' he said, shuddering, 'it's most beastly stuff. It's that nasty, sticky, sweet kind.'

'It will soon be over, father,' John said cheerily, and then in rushed Wendy with the medicine in a glass.

'Michael first,' Mr Darling said doggedly.

'Father first,' said Michael, who was of a suspicious nature.

'I shall be sick, you know,' Mr Darling said threateningly.

'Come on, father,' said John.

'Hold your tongue, John,' his father rapped out.

Wendy was quite puzzled. 'I thought you took it quite easily, father.'

18

'That's not the point,' he retorted. 'The point is, that there is more in my glass than in Michael's spoon. It isn't fair.'

'Father's a cowardy custard,' said Michael.

'So are you a cowardy custard.'

'I'm not frightened.'

'Neither am I frightened.'

'Well, then, take it.'

'Well, then, you take it.'

Wendy had a splendid idea. 'Why not both take it at the same time?'

'Certainly,' said Mr Darling. 'Are you ready, Michael?'

Wendy gave the word, one, two, three, and Michael took his medicine, but Mr Darling slipped his behind his back.

There was a yell of rage from Michael, and 'O father!' Wendy exclaimed.

'What do you mean, "O father"?' Mr Darling demanded. 'Stop that row, Michael. I meant to take mine, but I – I missed it.'

It was dreadful the way all the three were looking at him, just as if they did not admire him. 'Look here, all of you,' he said entreatingly, as soon as Nana had gone into the bathroom. 'I have just thought of a splendid joke. I shall pour my medicine into Nana's bowl, and she will drink it, thinking it is milk! Nana, good dog,' he said, calling her, 'I have put a little milk into your bowl, Nana.'

19

Nana wagged her tail, ran to the medicine, and began lapping it. Then she gave Mr Darling *such* a look, and crept into her kennel.

Mrs Darling returned with the chocolate and smelt the bowl. 'O George,' she said, 'it's your medicine!'

'It was only a joke,' he roared, while she comforted her boys, and Wendy hugged Nana. 'Much good,' he said bitterly, 'my wearing myself to the bone trying to be funny in this house.'

And still Wendy hugged Nana. 'That's right,' he shouted, 'Coddle her! Nobody coddles me. Oh dear no! But I refuse to allow that dog to lord it in my nursery for an hour longer.'

Nana ran to him, but he waved her back. 'The proper place for you is the yard,' he cried, 'and there you go to be tied up this instant.'

'George, George,' Mrs Darling whispered, 'remember what I told you about that boy.'

Alas, he would not listen, but dragged Nana from the room. He was ashamed of himself, and yet he did it. When he had tied her up in the backyard, he went and sat in the passage, with his knuckles to his eyes.

In the meantime Mrs Darling had put the children to bed in unwonted silence and lit the candles in their night-lights. They could hear Nana barking and John whimpered, 'It is because he is chaining her up in the yard,' but Wendy was wiser.

'That is not Nana's unhappy bark,' she said, 'that is her bark when she smells danger.'

'Danger! Are you sure, Wendy?'

'Oh yes.'

Mrs Darling quivered and went to the window. It was securely fastened. She looked out, and the night was peppered with stars. They were crowding round the house, as if curious to see what was to take place there. She did not notice this, yet a nameless fear clutched at her heart and made her cry, 'Oh, how I wish that I wasn't going to a party tonight!'

But she went. No. 27 was only a few yards distant, and as soon as the door closed on Mr and Mrs Darling there was a commotion in the heavens, and the smallest of the stars in the Milky Way screamed out: 'Now, Peter!'

Come Away, Come Away!

THE NIGHT-LIGHTS in the children's bedroom blinked and went out. There was another light in the room now, a thousand times brighter than the night-lights, and in the time we have taken to say this, it has been in all the drawers in the room, looking for Peter's shadow, rummaged the wardrobe and turned every pocket inside out. It was not really a light; when it came to rest for a second you saw it was a fairy, no longer than your hand.

A moment after the fairy's entrance, the window was blown open and Peter Pan dropped in. 'Tinker Bell,' he called softly, after making sure the children were asleep. 'Tink, where are you? Oh, do come out and tell me, do you know where they put my shadow?'

The loveliest tinkle as of golden bells answered him. It is the fairy language. Tink said that the shadow was in the chest of drawers. Peter jumped at it, scattering the contents of the drawers with both hands. In a moment he had recovered his shadow, and in his delight he forgot that he had shut Tinker Bell up in the drawer.

If he thought at all, but I don't believe he ever thought, it was that he and his shadow, when brought near each other, would join like drops of water; and when they did not he was appalled. He tried to stick it on with soap from the bathroom, but that also failed. A shudder passed through Peter, and he sat on the floor and cried.

His sobs woke Wendy, and she sat up in bed. She was not alarmed to see a stranger crying on the nursery floor; she was only pleasantly interested.

'Boy,' she said courteously, 'why are you crying?'

Peter could be exceedingly polite also, having learned the grand manner from the fairies, and he bowed to her beautifully. She was much pleased, and bowed beautifully to him from the bed.

'What's your name?' he asked.

'Wendy Moira Angela Darling,' she replied with some satisfaction. 'What is your name?'

'Peter Pan.'

'Is that all?'

'Yes,' he said sharply. He felt for the first time that it was a shortish name.

21

She asked him where he lived.

'Second to the right,' said Peter, 'and then straight on till morning.'

'What a funny address!'

'No, it isn't,' he said.

'I mean,' Wendy said nicely, remembering that she was hostess, 'is that what they put on the letters?'

'Don't get any letters,' he said contemptuously.

'But your mother gets letters?'

'Don't have a mother,' he said. Not only had he no mother, but he had not the slightest desire to have one. He thought them very over-rated persons. Wendy, however, felt that this was a tragedy.

'O Peter, no wonder you were crying,' she said, and got up and ran to him.

22

'I wasn't crying about mothers,' he said rather indignantly. 'I was crying because I can't get my shadow to stick on. Besides, I wasn't crying.'

'Your shadow has come off?'

'Yes.'

'How awful!' she said, but she could not help smiling when she saw that he had been trying to stick it on with soap. How exactly like a boy!

Fortunately she knew at once what to do. 'I shall sew it on for you,' she said, and she got out her workbasket and sewed the shadow to Peter's foot. Soon it was behaving properly, though still a little creased.

'Perhaps I should have ironed it,' Wendy said thoughtfully. But Peter was jumping about in the wildest glee. He had already forgotten that he owed his bliss to Wendy. 'How clever I am,' he crowed rapturously, 'oh, the cleverness of me!'

It is humiliating to have to confess that this conceit of Peter was one of his most fascinating qualities. To put it with brutal frankness, there never was a cockier boy.

But for the moment Wendy was shocked. 'Your conceit!' she exclaimed. 'Of course I did nothing!'

'You did a little,' Peter said carelessly, and continued to dance.

'A little!' she replied with hauteur; 'if I am no use I can at least withdraw,' and she sprang in the most dignified way into bed and covered her face with the blankets.

To make her look up he pretended to be going away, and when this failed he sat on the end of the bed and tapped her gently with his foot. 'Wendy,' he said, 'don't withdraw. I can't help crowing, Wendy, when I'm pleased with myself.' Still she would not look up, though she was listening eagerly. 'Wendy,' he continued, 'Wendy, one girl is more use than twenty boys.'

Wendy peeped out of the bedclothes. 'Do you really think so, Peter?'

'Yes, I do.'

'I think it's perfectly sweet of you,' she declared, 'and I'll get up again.' She sat with him on the side of the bed and said she would give him a kiss if he liked. Peter did not know what she meant, and he held out his hand expectantly.

'Surely you know what a kiss is?' she asked.

'I shall know when you give it to me,' he replied stiffly; and not to hurt his feelings she gave him a thimble.

'Now,' said he, 'shall I give you a kiss?' She replied with a slight primness, 'If you please,' but he merely dropped an acorn button into her hand.

She said nicely that she would wear it on a chain around her neck. It was lucky she did, for it was afterwards to save her life.

'Peter, how old are you?' she asked.

'I don't know,' he replied uneasily, 'but I am quite young. I ran away the day I was born.'

'Why?'

'It was because I heard father and mother talking about what I was to be when I became a man. I don't want ever to be a man,' he said with passion. 'I want always to be a little boy and to have fun. So I ran away to Kensington Gardens and lived a long time among the fairies.'

She gave him a look of the most intense admiration, and he thought it was because he had run away, but it was really because he knew fairies. She poured out questions about them, to his surprise, for he thought they were rather a nuisance. Still, he liked them on the whole, and he told her about the beginning of fairies.

'You see, Wendy, when the first baby laughed for the first time, its laugh broke into a thousand pieces, and they all went skipping about, and that was the beginning of fairies.'

Tedious talk this, but Wendy liked it.

'And so,' he went on good-naturedly, 'there ought to be one fairy for every boy and girl.'

'Ought to be? Isn't there?'

'No. You see, children know such a lot now, they soon don't believe in fairies, and every time a child says, "I don't believe in fairies," there is a fairy somewhere that falls down dead.'

Really, he thought they had now talked enough about fairies, and it struck him that Tinker Bell was keeping very quiet. 'I can't think where she has gone to,' he said, rising, and he called Tink by name. Wendy's heart went flutter with a sudden thrill.

'Peter!' she cried, clutching him, 'you don't mean to tell me there is a fairy in this room!'

'She was here just now,' he said a little impatiently. 'You don't hear her, do you?'

A sound like a tinkle of bells came from the chest of drawers, and Peter made a merry face. 'Wendy,' he whispered gleefully, 'I do believe I shut her up in the drawer!'

He let poor Tink out of the drawer, and she flew about the room screaming with fury.

'O Peter,' Wendy cried, 'if she would only stand still and let me see her!'

'They hardly ever stand still,' he said, but for one moment Wendy saw the romantic figure come to rest on the cuckoo clock. 'O the lovely!' she cried, though Tink's face was still distorted with passion.

'Tink,' said Peter amiably, 'this lady says she wishes you were her fairy.'

Tinker Bell answered insolently.

'What does she say, Peter?'

He had to translate. 'She is not very polite. She says you are a great ugly girl, and that she is my fairy.'

He tried to argue with Tink. 'You know you can't be my fairy, Tink, because I am a gentleman and you are a lady.'

To this Tink replied in these words, 'You silly ass,' and disappeared into the bathroom.

They were sitting together in the armchair by this time, and Wendy plied him with more questions.

'Where do you live now?'

'With the lost boys.'

'Who are they?'

'They are the children who fall out of their prams when no one's looking. If they are not claimed in seven days they are sent far away to the Never Land. I'm their captain.'

'What fun it must be!'

'Yes,' said cunning Peter, 'but we are rather lonely. You see we have no female companionship.'

'Are none of the others girls?'

'Oh no. Girls, you know, are much too clever to fall out of their prams.'

This flattered Wendy immensely. 'I think,' she said, 'it is perfectly lovely the way you talk about girls. John there just despises us.'

For reply Peter rose and tumbled John out of bed. This seemed to Wendy rather forward for the first meeting, and she told him with spirit that he was not captain in her house. However, John continued to sleep placidly on the floor. 'I know you meant to be kind,' she said, relenting, 'so you may give me a kiss.'

For a moment she had forgotten his ignorance about kisses. 'I thought you would want it back,' he said a little bitterly, and offered to return the thimble.

'Oh dear,' said Wendy, 'I don't mean a kiss, I mean a thimble.'

'What's that?'

'It's like this.' She kissed him.

'Funny!' said Peter gravely. 'Now shall I give you a thimble?'

'If you wish to,' said Wendy.

Peter thimbled her, and immediately she screeched. 'What is it, Wendy?'

'It was exactly as if someone were pulling my hair.'

'That must have been Tink. I never knew her so naughty before.'

And indeed Tink was darting about again, using offensive language.

'She says she will do that to you, Wendy, every time I give you a thimble.'

'But why?'

'Why, Tink?'

Again Tink replied, 'You silly ass.' Peter could not understand why, but Wendy understood, and she was just slightly disappointed when he admitted that he came to the children's window not to see her but to listen to stories.

'You see, I don't know any stories. None of the lost boys knows any stories.'

'How perfectly awful,' Wendy said.

'Do you know,' Peter asked, 'why swallows build in the eaves of houses? It is to listen to the stories. O Wendy, your mother was telling you such a lovely story.'

'Which story was it?'

'About the prince who couldn't find the lady who wore the glass slipper.'

'Peter,' said Wendy excitedly, 'that was Cinderella, and he found her, and they lived happily ever after.'

Peter was so glad that he jumped up at once.

'Where are you going?' she cried with misgiving.

'To tell the other boys.'

'Don't go, Peter,' she entreated, 'I know such lots of stories.'

Those were her precise words, so there can be no denying that it was she who first tempted him.

He came back, and there was a greedy look in his eyes now which ought to have alarmed her, but did not.

'Wendy, do come with me and tell the other boys.'

'Oh dear, I can't. Think of mummy! Besides, I can't fly.'

'I'll teach you. I'll teach you how to jump on the wind's back.'

'Oo!' she exclaimed rapturously.

'Wendy, Wendy, when you are sleeping in your silly bed you might be flying about with me saying funny things to the stars. And, Wendy, there are mermaids.'

'Oh,' cried Wendy, 'to see a mermaid!'

Peter had become frightfully cunning. 'Wendy,' he said, 'how we should all respect you. And you could tuck us in at night. And you could darn our clothes, and make pockets for us. None of us has any pockets.'

How could she resist? 'Of course it's awfully fascinating!' she cried. 'Peter, would you teach John and Michael to fly too?'

'If you like,' he said indifferently, and she ran to John and Michael and shook them. 'Wake up,' she cried, 'Peter Pan has come and he is to teach us to fly.'

John rubbed his eyes. 'Then I shall get up,' he said. Of course he was on the floor already. 'Hallo,' he said, 'I am up!'

Michael was up by this time also, but Peter suddenly signed silence. All was as still as salt. Then everything was right. No, stop! Everything was wrong. Nana, who had been barking distressfully all the evening, was quiet now. It was her silence they had heard.

Nana had been straining and straining on her chain until at last she broke it. In another moment she had burst into the dining room of No. 27 and flung her paws to heaven. Mr and Mrs Darling knew at once that something terrible was happening in the children's room, and without a goodbye to their hostess they rushed into the street.

In the meantime, Peter was teaching the children to fly. 'How sweet!' cried Wendy, watching him.

'Yes, I'm sweet, oh, I am sweet!' said Peter, forgetting his manners again.

It looked delightfully easy, and they tried it first from the floor and then from the beds, but they always went down instead of up.

'I say, how do you do it?' asked John, rubbing his knee.

'You just think lovely wonderful thoughts,' Peter explained, 'and they lift you up in the air.'

He showed them again.

'I've got it now, Wendy!' cried John, but he soon found he had not. Not one of them could fly an inch, though even Michael could read words of two syllables, and Peter did not know A from Z.

Of course Peter had been trifling with them, for no one can fly unless the fairy dust has been blown on him. Fortunately, one of his hands was messy with it, and he blew some on each of them, with the most superb results.

'Now just wriggle your shoulders this way,' he said, 'and let go.'

They were all on the beds, and gallant Michael let go first. Immediately he was borne across the room.

'I flewed!' he screamed while still in mid-air.

John let go, and met Wendy near the bathroom.

'Look at me!'

'Look at me!'

They were not nearly so elegant as Peter, they could not help kicking a little, but their heads were bobbing against the ceiling, and there is almost nothing so delicious as that.

Up and down they went, and round and round. 'Heavenly!' said Wendy.

'I say,' cried John, 'why shouldn't we all go out?'

Of course it was to this that Peter had been luring them. But Wendy hesitated.

'Mermaids!' said Peter again.

'Oo!'

'And there are pirates.'

'Pirates,' cried John, seizing his Sunday top-hat, 'let us go at once.'

It was just at this moment that Mr and Mrs Darling and Nana hurried out of No. 27. They ran into the middle of the street to look up at the nursery window; and yes, it was still shut, but the room was ablaze with light, and most heart-gripping sight of all, they could see in shadow on the curtain three little figures in night attire circling round and round, not on the floor but in the air.

Not three figures, four!

In a tremble they opened the street door. Mr Darling would have rushed upstairs, but Mrs Darling signed to him to go softly. She even tried to make her heart go softly.

They would have reached the children's room in time had it not been that the little stars were watching them. Once again the stars blew the window open, and the smallest star of all called out: 'Look out, Peter!'

Then Peter knew there was not a moment to lose. 'Come,' he ordered, and soared out at once into the night, followed by John and Michael and Wendy.

Mr and Mrs Darling and Nana rushed into the room too late. The birds had flown.

The Flight

SECOND TO THE RIGHT, and straight on till morning.'

That, Peter had told Wendy, was the way to the Never Land; but even birds, carrying maps and consulting them at windy corners, could not have sighted it with these instructions. Peter, you see, just said anything that came into his head.

At first his companions trusted him implicitly, and so great were the delights of flying that they wasted time circling round church spires or any other tall objects on the way that took their fancy. Soon they were flying over the sea.

Sometimes it was dark and sometimes light, and now they were very cold and again too warm. They were certainly sleepy, and that was a danger, for the moment they dropped off, down they fell. The awful thing was that Peter thought this was funny.

'There he goes again!' he would cry gleefully, as Michael suddenly dropped like a stone.

'Save him, save him!' cried Wendy, looking with horror at the cruel sea far below. Eventually Peter would dive through the air, and catch Michael just before he could strike the sea, and it was lovely the way he did it; but he always waited till the last moment, and you felt it was his cleverness that interested him and not the saving of human life.

Peter could sleep in the air without falling, by merely lying on his back and floating, but this was, partly at least, because he was so light that if you got behind him and blew he went faster.

'Do be polite to him,' Wendy whispered to John, when they were playing 'Follow My Leader'.

'Then tell him to stop showing off,' said John.

'You must be nice to him,' Wendy impressed on her brothers. 'What would we do if he were to leave us?'

'We could go back,' Michael said.

'How could we ever find our way back without him?'

'Well, then, we could go on,' said John.

'That is the awful thing, John. We should have to go on, for we don't know how to stop.'

This was true; Peter had forgotten to show them how to stop.

John said that if the worst came to the worst, all they had to do was to go straight on, for the world was round, and so in time they must come back to their window.

'But see how we bump against clouds and things if he is not near to give us a hand,' said Wendy.

Indeed they were constantly bumping. They could now fly strongly, though they still kicked far too much; but if they saw a cloud in front of them, the more they tried to avoid it, the more certainly did they bump into it.

Peter was not with them for the moment, and they felt rather lonely up there by themselves. He could go so much faster than they that he would suddenly shoot out of sight, to have some adventure in which they had no share. He would come down laughing over something fearfully funny he had been saying to a star, but he had already forgotten what it was, or he would come up with mermaid scales sticking to him, and yet not be able to say for certain what had been happening. It was really rather irritating to children who had never seen a mermaid.

'And if he forgets them so quickly,' Wendy argued, 'how can we expect that he will go on remembering us?'

For sometimes, when he returned, he did not remember them, at least not well. Wendy was sure of it. She saw recognition come into his eyes as he was about to pass the time of day and go on; once even, she had to tell him her name.

He was very sorry. 'I say, Wendy,' he whispered to her, 'always if you see me forgetting you, just keep on saying, "I'm Wendy", and then I'll remember.'

Of course this was rather unsatisfactory. However, to make amends he showed them how to lie out flat on a strong wind that was going their way, and this was such a pleasant change that they tried it several times and found they could sleep thus with security. Indeed they would have slept longer, but Peter tired quickly of sleeping, and soon he would cry in his captain voice, 'We get off here.'

So, with occasional tiffs but on the whole rollicking, they drew near the Never Land; not perhaps so much owing to the guidance of Peter or Tink as because the island was out looking for them. It is only thus that anyone may sight those magic shores.

'There it is,' said Peter calmly.

31

A million golden arrows were pointing out the island to the children, all directed by their friend the sun, who wanted them to be sure of their way before leaving them for the night.

Wendy and John and Michael stood on tiptoe in the air to get their first sight of the island. Strange to say, they all recognized it at once.

'John, there's the lagoon.'

'Wendy, look at the turtles burying their eggs in the sand.'

'Look, Michael, there's your cave.'

'There's my boat, John, with her sides stove in.'

'No it isn't. Why, we burned your boat.'

'That's her, at any rate. I say, John, I see the smoke of the redskin camp.'

Peter was a little annoyed with them for knowing so much; but if he wanted to lord it over them his triumph was at hand, for suddenly fear fell upon them.

It came as the arrows went, leaving the island in gloom.

In the old days at home the Never Land had always begun to look a little dark and threatening by bedtime. The unexplored patches arose in it and spread; black shadows moved about in them; the roar of the beasts of prey was quite different now, and above all, you lost the certainty that you would win. You were quite glad the night-lights were on.

Of course the Never Land had been make-believe in those days; but it was real now, and there were no night-lights, and it was getting darker every moment, and where was Nana?

They had been flying apart, but they huddled close to Peter now. His careless manner had gone at last, his eyes were sparkling, a tingle went through him every time they touched his body. Nothing horrid was visible in the air, yet their progress had become slow and laboured, exactly as if they were pushing their way through hostile forces.

Sometimes Peter poised himself in the air, listening intently with his hand to his ear, and again he would stare down with eyes so bright that they seemed to bore two holes to earth. Having done these things, he went on again.

His courage was almost appalling. 'Do you want an adventure now,' he said casually to John, 'or would you like to have your tea first?'

Wendy said 'tea first' quickly, but the braver John hesitated.

'What kind of adventure?' he asked cautiously.

'There's a pirate asleep in the pampas just beneath us,' Peter told him. 'If you like, we'll go down and kill him.'

'Suppose,' said John a little huskily, 'he were to wake up?'

Peter spoke indignantly. 'You don't think I would kill him while he was sleeping! I would wake him first, and then kill him. That's the way I always do.'

'I say! Do you kill many?'

'Tons.'

John said 'how ripping', but decided to have tea first. He asked if there were many pirates on the island just now, and Peter said he had never known so many.

'Who is captain now?'

'Hook,' answered Peter; and his face became very stern as he said that hated word.

'Jas. Hook?'

'Aye.'

Then indeed Michael began to cry, and even John could speak in gulps only, for they knew Hook's reputation.

'He was Blackbeard's bo'sun,' John whispered huskily. 'He is the worst of them all. He is the only man of whom Barbecue was afraid.'

'That's him,' said Peter.

'What is he like? Is he big?'

'He is not so big as he was.'

'How do you mean?'

'I cut off a bit of him.'

'You!'

'Yes, me,' said Peter sharply.

'But, I say, what bit?'

'His right hand.'

'Then he can't fight now?'

'Oh, can't he just! He has an iron hook instead of a right hand, and he claws with it.'

'Claws!'

'I say, John,' said Peter, 'there is one thing that every boy who serves under me has to promise, and so must you.'

John paled.

'It is this. If we meet Hook in open fight, you must leave him to me.'

'I promise,' John said loyally.

Tink could not fly so slowly as they, and so she had to go round and round them in a circle in which they moved as in a halo. Wendy quite liked it, until Peter pointed out the drawback.

'She tells me,' he said, 'that the pirates sighted us before the darkness came, and got Long Tom out.'

'The big gun?'

'Yes. And of course they must see her light, and if they guess we are near it they are sure to let fly.'

'Tell her to go away at once, Peter,' the three cried simultaneously, but he refused.

'She is rather frightened,' he replied stiffly. 'You don't think I would send her away all by herself when she's frightened!'

'Then tell her,' Wendy begged, 'to put out her light.'

'She can't put it out. That is about the only thing fairies can't do. It just goes out of itself when she falls asleep, same as the stars. If only one of us had a pocket, we could carry her in it.'

However, they had set off in such a hurry that there was not a pocket between the four of them.

He had a happy idea. John's hat!

Tink agreed to travel by hat if it was carried in the hand. Wendy took it, and this, as we shall see, led to mischief, for Tinker Bell hated to be under an obligation to Wendy.

In the black topper the light was completely hidden, and they flew on in silence. It was the stillest silence they had ever known. To Michael the loneliness was dreadful. 'If only something would make a sound!' he cried.

As if in answer to his request, the air was rent by the most tremendous crash he had ever heard. The pirates had fired Long Tom at them.

When at last the heavens were steady again, John and Michael found themselves alone in the darkness. Peter had been carried by the wind of the shot far out to sea, while Wendy was blown upwards.

It would have been well for Wendy if at that moment she had dropped the hat.

I don't know whether the idea came suddenly to Tink, or whether she had planned it on the way, but she at once popped out of the hat and began to lure Wendy to her destruction.

Tink was not all bad: or, rather, she was all bad just now, but, on the other hand, sometimes she was all good. Fairies have to be one thing or the other, because being so small they unfortunately have room for one feeling only at a time. At present she was full of jealousy of Wendy. What she said in her lovely tinkle Wendy could not of course understand, but she flew back and forward, plainly meaning 'Follow me, and all will be well.'

What else could poor Wendy do? She did not know that Tink hated her. And so, bewildered, and now staggering in her flight, she followed Tink to her doom.

The Island Come True

FEELING THAT PETER was on his way back, the Never Land had woken into life. The lost boys were out looking for their captain. There were six of them tramping through the sugar-cane, counting the Twins as two. They wore the skins of bears slain by themselves, in which they were so round and furry that when they fell they rolled. They have therefore become very sure-footed.

In the lead is Tootles, not the least brave but the most unfortunate of all that gallant band. He had been in fewer adventures than any of them, because the big things constantly happened just when he had stepped round the corner. All would be quiet, he would take the opportunity of going off to gather a few sticks for firewood, and then when he returned the others would be sweeping up the blood. This ill luck, instead of souring his nature, had sweetened it, so that he was quite the humblest of the boys. Poor kind Tootles, there is danger in the air for you tonight. The fairy Tink, who is bent on mischief this night, is looking for a tool, and she thinks you the most easily tricked of the boys. Beware Tinker Bell.

Next comes Nibs, the gay and debonair, followed by Slightly, who cuts whistles out of the trees and dances to his own tunes. Curly is fourth, and last come the Twins, who cannot be described because we should be sure to be describing the wrong one.

The pirates follow on the track of the lost boys. They are singing their dreadful song:

> 'Avast belay, yo ho, heave to,
> A-pirating we go,
> And if we're parted by a shot
> We're sure to meet below!'

A more villainous-looking lot never hung in a row on Execution Dock. Here, a little in advance, ever and again with his head to the ground listening, his great arms bare, pieces of eight in his ears as ornaments, is the handsome Italian Cecco. That gigantic black man behind him has had many names since he dropped the one with which mothers still terrify their children on the banks of the Guidjo-mo. Here is Bill Jukes, every inch of him tattooed; and Cookson, said to be Black Murphy's brother; and Gentleman Starkey, still dainty in his ways of killing; and the Irish bo'sun Smee, an oddly genial man who stabbed, so to speak, without offence; and Noodler, and many another ruffian long known and feared on the Spanish Main.

In the midst of them, the blackest and largest jewel in that dark setting, reclined James Hook, or, as he wrote himself, Jas. Hook. He lay at his ease in a rough chariot drawn and propelled by his men, and instead of a right hand he had the iron hook with which ever and anon he encouraged them to increase their pace. As dogs this terrible man treated and addressed them, and as dogs they obeyed him. In person he was cadaverous and blackavized, and his hair was dressed in long curls, which at a little distance looked like black candles, and gave a singularly threatening expression to his handsome countenance. His eyes were of the blue of the forget-me-not, and of a profound melancholy, save when he was plunging his hook into you, at which time two red spots appeared in

them and lit them up horribly. In manner, something of the great lord still clung to him, so that he even ripped you up with a dashing air. He was never more sinister than when he was most polite, which is probably the truest test of breeding; and the elegance of his diction, even when he was swearing, no less than the distinction of his demeanour, showed him one of a different caste from his crew. A man of indomitable courage, it was said of him that the only thing he shied at was the sight of his own blood, which was thick and of an unusual colour. In his mouth he had a cigar-holder designed by himself which enabled him to smoke two cigars at once. But undoubtedly the grimmest part of him was his iron claw.

Such is the terrible man against whom Peter Pan is pitted. Which will win?

On the trail of the pirates, stealing noiselessly down the war-path, which is not visible to inexperienced eyes, come the redskins. They carry tomahawks and knives, and their naked bodies gleam with paint and oil. Strung around them are scalps, of boys as well as of pirates, for these are the Piccaninny tribe, and not to be confused with the softer-hearted Delawares or the Hurons. In the van is Great Big Little Panther, a brave of so many scalps that they somewhat impede his progress. Bringing up the rear, the place of greatest danger, comes Tiger Lily, proudly erect, a princess in her own right, the belle of the Piccaninnies.

Observe how they pass over fallen twigs without making the slightest noise. The only sound to be heard is their somewhat heavy breathing. The fact is that they are all a little fat just now, after some heavy feasting while Peter Pan was away, but they will work this off.

The redskins disappear as they have come, like shadows, and their place is

40

taken by the beasts, a great and motley procession: lions, tigers, bears, and the innumerable smaller savage things that flee from them, for every kind of beast, and, more particularly, all the man-eaters, live cheek by jowl on the favoured island. Their tongues are hanging out. They are hungry tonight.

Last of all comes a gigantic crocodile. We shall see for whom it is looking presently.

The lost boys, growing tired, at last flung themselves down on the sward, close to their underground home.

'I do wish Peter would come back,' every one of them said nervously, though they were all larger than their captain.

'I am the only one who is not afraid of the pirates,' Slightly said in the tone that prevented his being a general favourite, 'but I wish he would come back and tell us whether he has heard anything more about Cinderella.'

They talked of Cinderella, and Tootles was confident that his mother must have been very like her.

It was only in Peter's absence that they could speak of mothers, the subject being forbidden by him as silly.

While they talked they heard a distant sound. It was the pirates' song:

> 'Yo ho, yo ho, the pirate life,
> The flag of skull and bones,
> A merry hour, a hempen rope,
> And hey for Davy Jones.'

At once the lost boys – but where are they? They are no longer there. Rabbits could not have disappeared more quickly.

41

They are already in their home under the ground, a very delightful residence of which we shall see a good deal presently. But how have they reached it? For there is no entrance to be seen. Look closely, however, and you may note that there are here seven large trees, each having in its hollow trunk a hole as large as a boy. These are the seven entrances to the home under the ground, for which Hook has been searching in vain these many moons. Will he find it tonight?

The pirates were searching diligently among the trees for the boys. 'Most of all,' Hook declared with passion, 'I want their captain, Peter Pan. 'Twas he cut off my arm.' He brandished the hook threateningly. 'I've waited long to shake his hand with this. Oh, I'll tear him.'

'And yet,' said Smee, 'I have often heard you say that hook was worth a score of hands, for combing the hair and other homely uses.'

'Aye,' the captain answered, 'if I was a mother I would pray to have my children born with this instead of that,' and he cast a look of pride upon his iron hand and one of scorn upon the other. Then again he frowned.

'Peter flung my arm,' he said, wincing, 'to a crocodile that happened to be passing by.'

'I have often,' said Smee, 'noticed your strange dread of crocodiles.'

'Not of crocodiles,' Hook corrected him, 'but of that one crocodile.' He lowered his voice. 'It liked my arm so much, Smee, that it has followed me ever since, from sea to sea and from land to land, licking its lips for the rest of me.'

'In a way,' said Smee, 'it's a sort of compliment.'

'I want no such compliments,' Hook barked petulantly. 'I want Peter Pan, who first gave the brute its taste for me.'

He sat down on a large mushroom, and now there was a quiver in his voice. 'Smee,' he said huskily, 'that crocodile would have had me before this, but by a lucky chance it swallowed a clock which goes tick tick inside it, and so before it can reach me I hear the tick, and bolt.' He laughed, but in a hollow way.

'Some day,' said Smee, 'the clock will run down, and then he'll get you.'

Hook wetted his dry lips. 'Aye,' he said, 'that's the fear that haunts me.'

Since sitting down he had felt curiously warm. 'Smee,' he said, 'this seat is hot.' He jumped up. 'Odds bobs, hammer and tongs, I'm burning.'

They examined the mushroom, which at once came away in their hands, for it had no root. Stranger still, smoke began at once to ascend. The pirates looked at each other, 'A chimney!' they both exclaimed.

They had indeed discovered the chimney of the home under the ground. It was the custom of the boys to stop it with a mushroom when enemies were in the neighbourhood.

Not only smoke came out of it. There came also children's voices, for so safe did the boys feel in their hiding-place that they were gaily chattering. The pirates listened grimly, and then replaced the mushroom. They looked around them and noted the holes in the seven trees.

'Did you hear them say Peter Pan's from home?' Smee whispered. Hook nodded. He stood for a long time lost in thought, and at last a curdling smile lit up his swarthy face. Smee had been waiting for it. 'Unrip your plan, captain,' he cried eagerly.

'To return to the ship,' Hook replied slowly through his teeth, 'and cook a large rich cake of a jolly thickness with green sugar on it. We will leave the cake on the shore of the Mermaids' Lagoon. These boys are always swimming about there, playing with the mermaids. They will find the cake and they will gobble it up, because, having no mother, they don't know how dangerous 'tis to eat rich damp cake.' He burst into laughter. 'Aha, they will die.'

'It's the wickedest, prettiest policy ever I heard of,' cried Smee, and in their exultation they danced and sang:

'Avast, belay, when I appear,
By fear they're overtook;
Naught's left upon your bones when you
Have shaken claws with Hook.'

They began the verse, but they never finished it, for another sound broke in and stilled them.

Tick tick tick tick.

Hook stood shuddering, one foot in the air. 'The crocodile,' he gasped, and bounded away, followed by his bo'sun.

Once more the boys emerged into the open. Nibs went off to make sure the pirates had gone, but soon returned with a rush. 'I have seen a wonderful thing,' he cried as they gathered round him eagerly. 'A great white bird. It is flying this way.'

'What kind of bird, do you think?'

'I don't know,' said Nibs, awestruck, 'but it looks so weary, and as it flies it moans, "Poor Wendy".'

'Poor Wendy?'

'I remember,' said Slightly instantly, 'there are birds called Wendies.'

'See, it comes,' cried Curly, pointing to Wendy in the heavens.

Wendy was now almost overhead, and they could hear her plaintive cry. But more distinct came the shrill voice of Tinker Bell. 'Peter Pan wants you to shoot the Wendy,' she cried.

It was not in their nature to question when Peter ordered. 'Let us do what Peter wishes,' cried the simple boys. 'Quick, bows and arrows.'

All but Tootles popped down their trees. He had a bow and arrow with him, and Tink noted it, and rubbed her little hands.

'Quick, Tootles, quick,' she screamed. 'Peter will be so pleased.'

Tootles excitedly fitted the arrow to his bow. 'Out of the way, Tink,' he shouted; and then he fired, and Wendy fluttered to the ground with an arrow in her breast.

44

The Little House

THE BOYS soon realized that a terrible mistake had been made. 'This is no bird,' said Slightly in a scared voice. 'I think it must be a lady.'

'And we have killed her,' Nibs said hoarsely.

'Now I see,' Curly said. 'Peter was bringing her to us.' He threw himself sorrowfully on the ground.

Tootles's face was very white. 'I did it,' he said, reflecting. 'When ladies used to come to me in dreams, I said, "Pretty mother, pretty mother." But when at last she really came, I shot her.'

It was at this tragic moment that they heard a sound which made the heart of every one of them rise to his mouth. They heard Peter crow.

'Greetings, boys,' he cried as he dropped in front of them. 'I am back. Why do you not cheer?'

The cheers would not come, but Peter overlooked it in his haste to tell the glorious tidings. 'Great news, boys! I have brought at last a mother for you all. Have you see her? She flew this way.'

'Peter,' said Tootles quietly, 'I will show her to you.'

They all stood back and let him see. 'She is dead,' Peter said uncomfortably. 'Perhaps she is frightened at being dead.'

He did not know what to do next. But there was the arrow. 'Whose arrow?' he demanded sternly.

'Mine, Peter,' said Tootles, on his knees.

'Oh, dastard hand,' Peter said, and he raised the arrow to use it as a dagger.

Twice did he raise the arrow, and twice did his hand fall. 'I cannot strike,' he said with awe, 'there is something stays my hand.'

All looked at him in wonder, save Nibs, who fortunately looked at Wendy.

'It is she,' he cried, 'the Wendy lady; see, her arm.'

Wonderful to relate, Wendy had raised her arm. Nibs bent over her and listened reverently. 'I think she said "Poor Tootles",' he whispered.

'She lives,' Peter said briefly.

Slightly cried instantly, 'The Wendy lady lives.'

Then Peter knelt beside her and found his button. You remember she had put it on a chain that she wore round her neck.

'See,' he said, 'the arrow struck against this. It is the kiss I gave her. It has saved her life.'

'I remember kisses,' Slightly interposed quickly, 'let me see it. Aye, that's a kiss.'

Peter did not hear him. He was begging Wendy to get better quickly, so that he could show her the mermaids. But the boys had to tell Peter of Tink's crime, and almost never had they seen him look so stern.

'Listen, Tinker Bell,' he cried. 'I am your friend no more. Begone from me for ever.'

She flew on to his shoulder and pleaded, but he brushed her off. Not until Wendy again raised her arm did he relent sufficiently to say, 'Well, not for ever, but for a whole week.'

As Wendy was still in a frightful faint and could not be moved, Peter decided to build a little house around her. 'Quick,' he ordered them, 'bring me each of

you the best of what we have. Gut our house. Be sharp.'

In a moment they were as busy as tailors the night before a wedding. They scurried this way and that, down for bedding, up for firewood, and while they were at it, who should appear but John and Michael. They were so tired they were falling asleep standing up, and they were very relieved to find Peter.

'Hallo, Peter,' they said.

'Hallo,' replied Peter amicably, though he had quite forgotten them. He was very busy at the moment measuring Wendy with his feet to see how large a house she would need. John and Michael watched him.

'Is Wendy asleep?' they asked.

'Yes.'

'John,' Michael proposed, 'let us wake her and get her to make supper for us.' But as he said it some of the other boys rushed up carrying branches for the building of the house. 'Look at them!' he cried.

'Curly,' said Peter in his most captainy voice, 'see that these boys help in the building of the house.'

The astounded brothers were dragged away to hack and hew and carry. 'Chairs and a fender first,' Peter ordered. 'Then we shall build the house around them.'

'Aye,' said Slightly, 'that is how a house is built. It all comes back to me.'

The wood was alive with the sound of axes; almost everything needed for a cosy dwelling already lay at Wendy's feet.

'If only we knew,' said Peter, 'the kind of house she likes best.'

'Peter,' shouted another, 'she is moving in her sleep.'

'Perhaps she is going to sing in her sleep,' said Peter. 'Wendy, sing the kind of house you would like to have.'

Immediately, without opening her eyes, Wendy began to sing:

> '*I wish I had a pretty house,*
> *The littlest ever seen,*
> *With funny little red walls*
> *And roof of mossy green.*'

They gurgled with joy at this, for by the greatest good luck the branches they had brought were sticky with red sap, and all the ground was carpeted with moss. They sang a song themselves as they rattled up the little house in next to no time.

The house was quite beautiful, and no doubt Wendy was very cosy within, though, of course, they could no longer see her. Peter strode up and down, ordering finishing touches. Nothing escaped his eagle eye. Just when it seemed absolutely finished he said, 'There's no knocker on the door.' Tootles gave the sole of his shoe, and it made an excellent knocker.

'There's no chimney,' Peter said. 'We must have a chimney.'

'It certainly does need a chimney,' said John importantly. This gave Peter an idea. He snatched the hat off John's head, knocked out the bottom and put the hat on the roof. The little house was so pleased to have such a capital chimney that, as if to say thank you politely, smoke immediately began to come out of the hat.

Now really and truly it was finished. Peter stepped up and knocked politely on the door.

The wood was as still as the children, not a sound to be heard except from Tinker Bell, who was watching from a branch and openly sneering.

The door opened and Wendy came out. They all whipped off their hats.

She looked properly surprised, and this was just how they had hoped she would look.

'Where am I?' she said.

Of course Slightly was the first to get his word in. 'Wendy lady,' he said rapidly, 'for you we built this house.'

'Oh, say you're pleased,' cried Nibs.

'Lovely, darling house,' said Wendy, and they were the very words they had hoped she would say.

'And we are your children,' cried the Twins.

Then all went on their knees, and holding out their arms cried, 'O Wendy lady, be our mother.'

'Ought I?' Wendy said, all shining. 'Of course it's frightfully fascinating, but you see I am only a little girl. I have no real experience.'

'That doesn't matter,' said Peter, as if he were the only person present who knew all about it, though he was really the one who knew least. 'What we need is just a nice motherly person.'

'Oh dear!' Wendy said, 'you see I feel that is exactly what I am.'

'It is, it is,' they all cried. 'We saw it at once.'

'Very well,' she said, 'I will do my best. Come inside at once, you naughty children. I am sure your feet are damp. And before I put you to bed I have just time to finish the story of Cinderella.'

In they went. I don't know how there was room for them, but you can squeeze very tight in the Never Land.

And that was the first of the many joyous evenings they had with Wendy. By and by she tucked them up in the great bed in the home under the trees, but she herself slept that night in the little house, and Peter kept watch outside with drawn sword, for the pirates could be heard carousing far away and the wolves were on the prowl.

After a time he fell asleep, and some unsteady fairies had to climb over him on their way home from a party. Any of the other boys obstructing the fairy path at night they would have mischiefed, but they just tweaked Peter's nose and passed on.

The Home Under the Ground

ONE OF THE first things Peter did next day was to measure Wendy and John and Michael for hollow trees. Peter measures you for your tree as carefully as for a suit of clothes, the only difference being that the clothes are made to fit you, while you have to be made to fit the tree.

Wendy and Michael fitted their trees at the first try, but John had to be altered a little.

After a few days' practice they could go up and down as gaily as buckets in a well. And how ardently they grew to love their home under the ground; especially Wendy. It consisted of one large room, as all houses should do, with a floor in which you could dig if you wanted to go fishing, and in this floor grew stout mushrooms of a charming colour, which were used as stools. A Never tree tried hard to grow in the centre of the room, but every morning they sawed the trunk through, level with the floor. By tea-time it was always about two feet high, and then they put a door on top of it, the whole thus becoming a table. As soon as they had cleared away, they sawed off the trunk again, and thus there was more room to play. There was an enormous fire-place which was in almost any part of the room where you cared to light it, and across this Wendy stretched strings, made of fibre, from which she suspended her washing. The bed was tilted against the wall by day, and let down at 6.30, when it filled nearly half the room; and all the boys except Michael slept in it, lying like sardines in a tin. There was a strict rule against turning round until one gave the signal, when all turned at once. Michael should have used it also; but Wendy would have a baby, and he was the littlest, and you know what women are, and the short and the long of it is that he was hung up in a basket.

Tinker Bell had her own private apartment in a recess in the wall, which could be shut off from the rest of the room by a tiny curtain.

It was all especially entrancing to Wendy, because those rampageous boys of hers gave her so much to do. Really there were whole weeks when, except perhaps with a stocking in the evening, she was never above ground. The cooking kept her nose to the pot. Their chief food was roasted bread-fruit, yams, coconuts, baked pig, mammee-apples, tappa rolls and bananas, washed down with calabashes of poe-poe; but you never exactly knew whether there would be

50

a real meal or just a make-believe, it all depended on Peter's whim.

Wendy's favourite time for sewing and darning was after they had all gone to bed. Then, as she expressed it, she had a breathing time for herself; and she occupied it in making new things for them, and putting double pieces on the knees, for they were all frightfully hard on their knees.

When she sat down to a basketful of their stockings, every heel with a hole in it, she would fling up her arms and exclaim, 'Oh dear, I am sure I sometimes think spinsters are to be envied.'

Her face beamed when she exclaimed this.

As time wore on did she think much about the beloved parents she had left behind her? This is a difficult question, because it is quite impossible to say how time does wear on in the Never Land. But I am afraid that Wendy did not really worry about her father and mother. She was absolutely confident that they would always keep the window open for her to fly back by, and this gave her complete ease of mind. What did disturb her at times was that John remembered his parents vaguely only, as people he had once known, while Michael was quite willing to believe that she was really his mother. These things scared her a little, and nobly anxious to do her duty, she tried to fix the old life in their minds by setting them examination papers on it, as like as possible to the ones she used to do at school. The other boys thought this awfully interesting and insisted on joining in.

They were the most ordinary questions. 'What was the colour of Mother's eyes? Which was taller, Father or Mother? Was Mother blonde or brunette? Answer all three questions if possible.' Or '(1) Describe Mother's laugh; (2) Describe Father's laugh; (3) Describe Mother's Party Dress; (4) Describe the Kennel and its Inmate.'

They were just everyday questions like these, and when you could not answer them you were told to make a cross and it was really dreadful what a number of crosses even John made.

Peter did not compete. For one thing he despised all mothers except Wendy, and for another he was the only boy on the island who could neither write nor spell, not the smallest word. He was above all that sort of thing.

By the way, the questions were all written in the past tense. What *was* the colour of Mother's eyes, and so on. Wendy, you see, had been forgetting too.

Adventures, of course, as we shall see, were of daily occurrence. Peter often went out alone, and when he came back you were never absolutely certain whether he had had an adventure or not. He might have forgotten it so completely that he said nothing about it; and then when you went out you found the body. And on the other hand, he might say a great deal about it, and yet you could not find the body. Sometimes he came home with his head bandaged, and then Wendy cooed over him and bathed it in lukewarm water, while he told a dazzling tale. But she was never quite sure. There were, however, many adventures which she knew to be true because she was in them herself, and there were still more that were at least partly true, for the other boys were in them and said they were wholly true.

Take the brush with the redskins at Slightly Gulch. It was a bloody affair, and especially interesting as showing one of Peter's peculiarities, which was that in the middle of a fight he would suddenly change sides. At the Gulch, when victory was still in the balance, he called out, 'I'm redskin today; what are you, Tootles?' And Tootles answered, 'Redskin; what are you Nibs?' and Nibs said, 'Redskin; what are you, Twin?' and so on; and they were all redskins. Of course this would have ended the fight had not the real redskins, fascinated by Peter's methods, agreed to be lost boys for that once, and so at it they all went again, more fiercely than ever.

Or we could tell of that cake the pirates cooked so that the boys might eat and perish; and how they placed it in one cunning spot after another; but always Wendy snatched it from the hands of her children, so that in time it lost its succulence, and became as hard as a stone, and was used as a missile, and Hook fell over it in the dark.

Or we might tell how Peter save Tiger Lily's life in the Mermaids' Lagoon, and so made her his ally . . .

The Mermaids' Lagoon

THE CHILDREN often spent long summer days on the Mermaids' Lagoon, swimming or floating most of the time, playing the mermaid games in the water and so forth. You must not think from this that the mermaids were on friendly terms with them; on the contrary, it was among Wendy's lasting regrets that all the time she was on the island she never had a civil word from them. When she stole softly to the edge of the lagoon she might see them by the score, especially on the Marooners' Rock, where they loved to bask, combing out their hair in a lazy way that quite irritated her; or she might even swim, on tiptoe as it were, to within a yard of them, but then they saw her and dived, probably splashing her with their tails, not by accident but intentionally.

They treated all the boys in the same way, except of course Peter, who chatted with them on Marooners' Rock by the hour, and sat on their tails when they got cheeky. He gave Wendy one of their combs.

Sometimes hundreds of mermaids would be playing in the lagoon at a time, and it was quite a pretty sight. But the moment the children tried to join in they had to play by themselves, for the mermaids immediately disappeared.

It must also have been rather pretty to see the children resting on a rock for half an hour after their midday meal. Wendy insisted on their doing this, and it had to be a real rest even though the meal was make-believe. So they lay there in the sun, and their bodies glistened in it, while she sat beside them and looked important.

It was one such day, and they were all on Marooners' Rock. The rock was not much larger than their great bed, but of course they all knew how not to take up much room, and they were dozing, while Wendy was busy stitching.

While she stitched a change came to the lagoon. Little shivers ran over it, and the sun went away and shadows stole across the water, turning it cold. When Wendy looked up, the lagoon that had always hitherto been such a laughing place seemed formidable and unfriendly.

There crowded upon her all the stories she had been told of Marooners' Rock, so called because evil captains put sailors on it and leave them there to drown. They drown when the tide rises, for then it is submerged.

Of course she should have roused the children at once; not merely because of the unknown that was stalking towards them, but because it was no longer good for them to sleep on a rock grown chilly. But she was a young mother and she did not know this. Even when she heard the sound of muffled oars, though her heart was in her mouth, she did not waken them. She stood over them to let them have their sleep out.

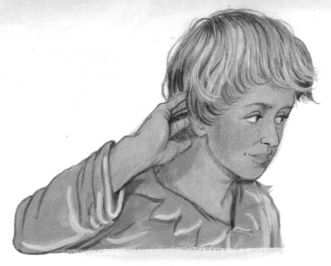

It was well for those boys then that there was one among them who could sniff danger even in his sleep. Peter sprang erect, as wide awake at once as a dog, and with one warning cry he roused the others.

He stood motionless, one hand to his ear.

'Pirates!' he cried. The others came closer to him. A strange smile was playing about his face, and Wendy saw it and shuddered. While that smile was on his face no one dared address him; all they could do was to stand ready to obey. The order came sharply and incisive.

'Dive!'

There was a gleam of legs, and instantly the lagoon seemed deserted. Marooners' Rock stood alone in the forbidding waters, as if it were itself marooned.

The boat drew nearer. It was the pirate dinghy, with three figures in her, Smee and Starkey, and the third a captive, no other than Tiger Lily. Her hands and ankles were tied and she knew what was to be her fate. She was to be left on the rock to perish. Yet her face was impassive; she was the daughter of a chief, she must die as a chief's daughter, it is enough.

In the gloom that they brought with them the two pirates did not see the rock till they crashed into it.

'Luff, you lubber,' cried an Irish voice that was Smee's. 'Here's the rock. Now then, what we have to do is to hoist the redskin on to it, and leave her there to drown.'

Quite near the rock, but out of sight, two heads were bobbing up and down, Peter's and Wendy's. Wendy was crying, for it was the first tragedy she had seen. Peter had seen many tragedies, but he had forgotten them all. He was less sorry than Wendy for Tiger Lily; it was two against one that angered him, and he meant to save her. An easy way would have been to wait until the pirates had gone, but he was never one to choose the easy way.

There was almost nothing he could not do, and he now imitated the voice of Hook.

'Ahoy there, you lubbers,' he called. It was a marvellous imitation.

'The captain,' said the pirates, staring at each other in surprise.

'He must be swimming out to us,' Starkey said, when they had looked for him in vain.

'We are putting the redskin on the rock,' Smee called out.

'Set her free,' came the astonishing answer.

'Free!'

'Yes, cut her bonds and let her go.'

'But, captain –'

'At once, d'ye hear,' cried Peter, 'or I'll plunge my hook in you.'

'This is queer,' Smee gasped.

'Better do what the captain orders,' said Starkey nervously.

'Aye, aye,' Smee said, and he cut Tiger Lily's cords. At once like an eel she slid between Starkey's legs into the water.

Of course Wendy was very elated over Peter's cleverness; but she knew that he would be elated also and very likely crow and thus betray himself, so at once her hand went out to cover his mouth. But it was stayed even in the act, for 'Boat ahoy!' rang over the lagoon in Hook's voice, and this time it was not Peter who had spoken. The real Hook was also in the water.

He was swimming to the boat, and as his men showed a light to guide him he had soon reached them. Wendy would have liked to swim away, but Peter would not budge. He was tingling with life and also top-heavy with conceit. 'Am I not a wonder, oh, I am a wonder!' he whispered to her; and though she thought so also, she was really glad for the sake of his reputation that no one heard him except herself.

Hook sat in the boat with his head on his hook, in a position of profound melancholy.

'Captain, is all well?' the pirates asked timidly, but he answered with a hollow moan.

'He sighs,' said Smee.

'He sighs again,' said Starkey.

'And yet a third time he sighs,' said Smee.

'What's up, captain?'

Then at last he spoke passionately. 'The game's up,' he cried, 'those boys have found a mother.'

Frightened though she was, Wendy swelled with pride.

'O evil day,' cried Starkey.

The ignorant Smee did not know what a mother was, but when that had been explained to him, he had a suggestion:

'Captain,' said he, 'could we not kidnap these boys' mother and make her our mother?'

'It is a princely scheme,' cried Hook, and at once it took practical shape in his great brain. 'We will seize the children and carry them to the boat: the boys we will make walk the plank, and Wendy shall be our mother. Do you agree, my bullies?'

'There is my hand on it,' they both said.

'And there is my hook. Swear.'

They all swore. By this time they were on the rock and suddenly Hook remembered Tiger Lily.

'Where is the redskin?' he demanded abruptly.

'That is all right, captain,' Smee answered complacently, 'we let her go.'

'Let her go!' cried Hook.

''Twas your own order,' the bo'sun faltered.

'You called over the water to us to let her go,' said Starkey.

'Brimstone and gall,' thundered Hook, 'what cozening is here?' His face had gone black with rage, but he saw that they believed their words, and he was startled. 'Lads,' he said, shaking a little, 'I gave no such order.'

'It is passing queer,' Smee said, and they all fidgeted uncomfortably. Hook raised his voice, but there was a quiver in it.

'Spirit that haunts this dark lagoon tonight,' he cried, 'dost hear me?'

Of course Peter should have kept quiet, but of course he did not. He immediately answered in Hook's voice:

'Odds, bobs, hammer and tongs, I hear you.'

Smee and Starkey clung to each other in terror, but Hook roared:

'Who are you, stranger, speak?'

'I am James Hook,' replied the voice, 'captain of the *Jolly Roger*.'

'You are not; you are not,' Hook cried hoarsely.

'Brimstone and gall,' the voice retorted, 'say that again, and I'll cast anchor in you.'

Hook tried a more ingratiating manner. 'If you are Hook,' he said almost humbly, 'come, tell me, who am I?'

'A codfish,' replied the voice, 'only a codfish.'

'A codfish!' Hook echoed blankly, and his men drew back from him.

'Have we been captained all this time by a codfish?' they muttered. 'It is lowering to our pride.'

Hook tried the guessing game. 'Hook,' he called, 'have you another voice?'

Now Peter could never resist a game, and he answered blithely in his own voice, 'I have.'

'And another name?'

'Aye, aye.'

'Vegetable?' asked Hook.

'No.'

'Mineral?'

'No.

'Animal?'

'Yes.'

'Man?'

'No!' This answer rang out scornfully.

'Boy?'

'Yes.'

'Wonderful boy?'

To Wendy's pain the answer rang out, 'Yes!'

But Hook was completely puzzled.

'Can't guess, can't guess,' crowed Peter. 'Do you give it up?'

Of course in his pride he was carrying the game too far, and the miscreants saw their chance.

'Yes, yes,' they answered eagerly.

'Well, then,' he cried, 'I am Peter Pan!'

'Pan!'

'Now we have him,' Hook shouted. 'Into the water, Smee. Starkey, mind the boat. Take him dead or alive.'

He leaped as he spoke, and simultaneously came the gay voice of Peter. 'Are you ready, boys?'

'Aye, aye,' from various parts of the lagoon.

'Then lam into the pirates.'

The fight was short and sharp. Here and there a head bobbed up in the water, and there was a flash of steel, followed by a cry or a whoop. In the confusion some struck at their own side. The sabre of Smee got Tootles in the fourth rib, but he was himself pinked in turn by Curly. Farther from the rock Starkey was pressing Slightly and the Twins hard.

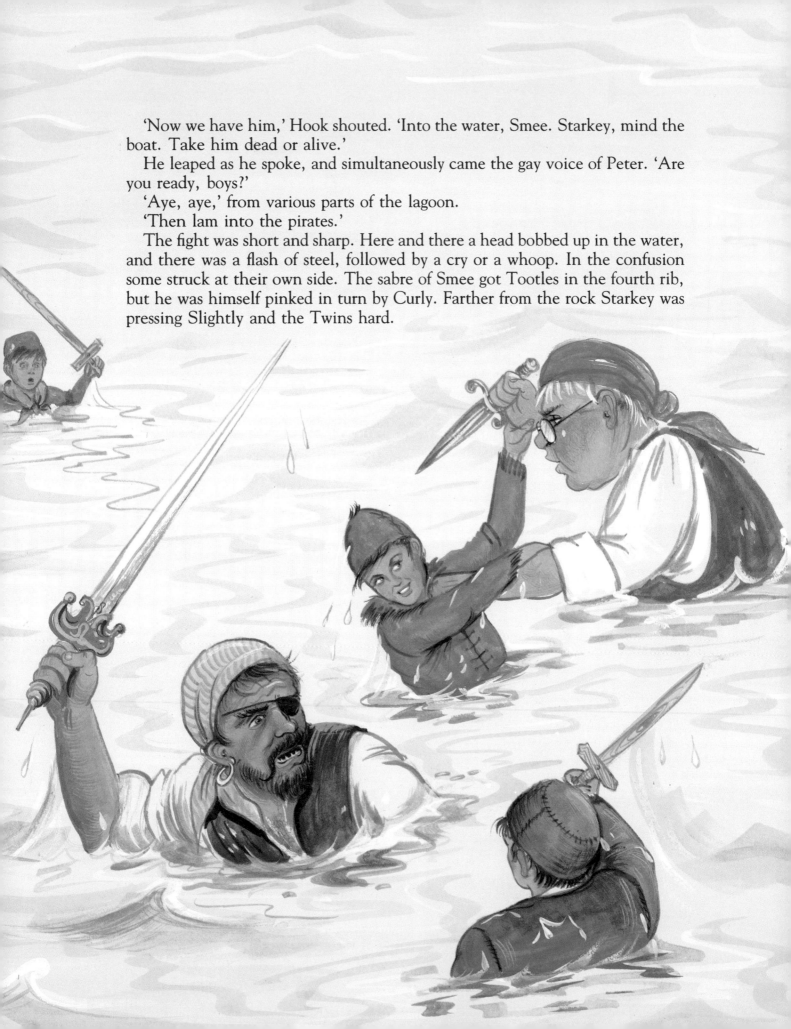

Where all this time was Peter? He was seeking bigger game.

The others were all brave boys, and they must not be blamed for backing from the pirate captain. His iron claw made a circle of dead water around him, from which they fled like frightened fishes.

But there was one who did not fear him: there was one prepared to enter that circle.

Strangely, it was not in the water that they met. Hook rose to the rock to breathe, and at the same moment Peter scaled it on the opposite side. The rock was slippery as a ball, and they had to crawl rather than climb. Neither knew that the other was coming. Each feeling for a grip met the other's arm: in surprise they raised their heads; their faces were almost touching; so they met.

Quick as thought Peter snatched a knife from Hook's belt and was about to drive it home when he saw that he was higher up on the rock than his foe. It would not have been fighting fair. He gave the pirate a hand to help him up.

Hook saw his intentions, and taking advantage of it, clawed him twice.

A few minutes afterwards the other boys saw Hook in the water striking wildly for the ship; no elation on his pestilent face now, only white fear, for the crocodile was in dogged pursuit of him. On ordinary occasions the boys would have swum alongside cheering; but now they were uneasy, for they had lost both Peter and Wendy, and were scouring the lagoon for them, calling them by name. They found the dinghy and went home in it, shouting, 'Peter, Wendy,' as they went, but no answer came save mocking laughter from the mermaids. 'They must be swimming back or flying,' the boys concluded. They chuckled, boylike, because they would be late for bed; and it was all Mother Wendy's fault!

When their voices died away there came cold silence over the lagoon, and then a feeble cry.

'Help, help!'

Two small figures were beating against the rock; the girl lay on the boy's arm. With a last effort Peter pulled her up the rock and then lay down beside her. The water was rising; he knew that they would soon be drowned, but he could do no more.

'We are on the rock, Wendy,' he said, 'but it is growing smaller. Soon the water will be over it.'

She did not understand. 'We must go,' she said almost brightly.

'Yes,' he answered faintly.

'Shall we swim or fly, Peter?'

'Do you think you could swim or fly as far as the island, Wendy, without my help?'

She had to admit that she was too tired.

He moaned.

'What is it?' she asked, anxious about him at once.

'I can't help you, Wendy. Hook wounded me. I can neither fly nor swim.'

'Do you mean we shall both be drowned?'

'Look how the water is rising.'

They put their hands over their eyes to shut out the sight. Then something brushed against Peter as light as a kiss, and stayed there, as if saying timidly, 'Can I be of any use?'

It was the tail of a kite, which Michael had made some days before. It had torn itself out of his hand and floated away.

'Michael's kite,' Peter said, pulling it towards him. 'It lifted Michael off the ground. Why should it not carry you?'

'Both of us!'

'It can't lift two; Michael and Curly tried.'

'Let us draw lots,' Wendy said bravely.

'And you a lady; never!' Already he had tied the tail around her. She clung to him; she refused to go without him; but with a, 'Goodbye, Wendy,' he pushed her from the rock; and in a few minutes she was borne out of his sight. Peter was alone on the lagoon.

The water was already lapping at Peter's feet when a Never bird came by on her floating nest, which was as big as a basin. She had seen Peter's plight and was ready to sacrifice her nest, eggs and all, to save him. As the nest bumped gently against the rock, she flew upwards, cooing a message to him. Peter, who knew the bird language, slipped into the nest, first removing the eggs and placing them in Starkey's hat. It had been left behind after the fight.

Using his shirt as a sail, Peter sailed safely to the shore, while the Never bird settled happily on Starkey's hat; it floated beautifully.

Great were the rejoicings when Peter reached the home under the ground, almost as soon as Wendy, who had been carried hither and thither by the kite. Every boy had adventures to tell; but perhaps the biggest adventure of all was that they were several hours late for bed. This so inflated them that they did various dodgy things to try to stay up still longer, such as demanding bandages; but Wendy, though glorying in having them all home again safe and sound, was scandalized by the lateness of the hour, and cried, 'To bed, to bed,' in a voice that had to be obeyed. Next day, however, she was awfully tender, and gave out bandages to every one. And they played till bedtime at limping about and carrying their arms in slings.

The Happy Home

ONE IMPORTANT result of the brush on the lagoon was that it made the redskins their friends. Peter had saved Tiger Lily from a dreadful fate, and now there was nothing she and her braves would not do for him. All night they sat above, keeping watch over the home under the ground and awaiting the big attack by the pirates which obviously could not be much longer delayed. Even by day they hung about, smoking the pipe of peace.

They called Peter the Great White Father, prostrating themselves before him; and he liked this tremendously, so that it was not really good for him.

'The Great White Father,' he would say to them in a very lordly manner, as they grovelled at his feet, 'is glad to see the Piccaninny warriors protecting his wigwam from the pirates.'

'Me Tiger Lily,' that lovely creature would reply. 'Peter Pan save me, me his velly nice friend. Me no let pirates hurt him.'

She was far too pretty to cringe in this way, but Peter thought it his due, and he would answer condescendingly, 'It is good. Peter Pan has spoken.'

Always when he said, 'Peter Pan has spoken,' it meant that they must now shut up, and they accepted it humbly in that spirit; but they were by no means so respectful to the other boys, whom they looked upon as just ordinary braves. They said, 'How-do?' to them, and things like that; and what annoyed the boys was that Peter seemed to think this all right.

Secretly Wendy sympathized with them a little, but she was far too loyal a housewife to listen to any complaints against father. 'Father knows best,' she always said, whatever her private opinion might be. Her private opinion was that the redskins should not call her squaw.

We have now reached the evening that was to be known among them as the Night of Nights, because of its adventures and their upshot. The day, as if quietly gathering its forces, had been almost uneventful, and now the redskins in their blankets were at their posts above, while, below, the children were having their evening meal; all except Peter, who had gone out to get the time. The way you got the time on the island was to find the crocodile, and then stay near him till the clock struck.

This meal happened to be a make-believe tea, and they sat round the board, guzzling in their greed; and really, what with their chatter and arguments, the noise, as Wendy said, was positively deafening. To be sure, she did not mind the noise, but she simply would not have them grabbing things, and then excusing themselves by saying that Tootles had pushed their elbow.

Afterwards, they played around Wendy while she sewed: such a group of happy faces and dancing limbs lit up by that romantic fire. It had become a very familiar scene this in the home under the ground, but we are looking on it for the last time.

There was a step above, and Wendy, you may be sure, was the first to recognize it.

'Children, I hear your father's step. He likes you to meet him at the door.'

Above, the redskins crouched before Peter.

'Watch well, braves. I have spoken.'

And then, as so often before, the merry children dragged him from his tree, As so often before, but never again.

He had brought nuts for the boys as well as the correct time for Wendy.

'Peter, you just spoil them, you know,' Wendy simpered.

The first Twin came to Peter. 'Father, we want to dance.'

They were told they could dance, as it was Saturday night, but they must put on their nighties first.

'Ah, old lady,' Peter said to Wendy, warming himself by the fire and looking down at her as she sat mending a sock, 'there is nothing more pleasant of an evening for you and me when the day's toil is over than to rest by the fire with the little ones near by.'

'It is sweet, Peter, isn't it?' Wendy said, frightfully gratified. 'Peter, I think Curly has your nose.'

'Michael takes after you.'

She went to him and put her hand on his shoulder. 'Dear Peter,' she said, 'with such a large family, of course, I have now passed my best, but you don't want to change me, do you?'

'No, Wendy.'

Certainly he did not want a change, but he looked at her uncomfortably, blinking like someone not sure whether he was awake or asleep.

'Peter, what is it?'

'I was just thinking,' he said, a little scared. 'It is only make-believe, isn't it, that I am their father?'

'Oh yes,' Wendy said primly.

'You see,' he continued apologetically, 'it would make me seem so old to be their real father.'

'But they are ours, Peter, yours and mine.'

'But not really, Wendy?' he asked anxiously.

'Not if you don't wish it,' she replied; and she distinctly heard his sigh of

relief. 'Peter,' she asked, trying to speak firmly, 'what are your exact feelings for me?'

'Those of a devoted son, Wendy.'

'I thought so,' she said, and went and sat by herself at the extreme end of the room.

'You are so queer,' he said, frankly puzzled, 'and Tiger Lily is just the same. There is something she wants to be to me, but she says it is not my mother.'

'No, indeed, it is not,' Wendy replied with frightful emphasis.

'Then what is it?'

'It isn't for a lady to tell.'

'Oh, very well,' Peter said, a little nettled. 'Perhaps Tinker Bell will tell me.'

'Oh yes, Tinker Bell will tell you,' Wendy retorted scornfully. 'She is an abandoned little creature.'

Here Tink, who was in her boudoir, eavesdropping, squeaked out something impudent.

'She says she glories in being abandoned,' Peter interpreted.

He had a sudden idea. 'Perhaps Tink wants to be my mother?'

'You silly ass!' cried Tinker Bell in a passion. She had said it so often that Wendy needed no translation.

66

'I almost agree with her,' Wendy snapped. Fancy Wendy snapping. But she had been much tried, and she little knew what was to happen before the night was out. If she had known she would not have snapped.

None of them knew. Perhaps it was best not to know. Their ignorance gave them one more glad hour; and as it was to be their last hour on the island, let us rejoice that there were sixty minutes in it. They sang and danced in their nightgowns. Such a deliciously creepy song it was, in which they pretended to be afraid of their own shadows; little knowing that so soon shadows would close in upon them, from whom they would shrink in real fear. So uproariously gay was the dance, and how they buffeted each other on the bed and out of it! It was a pillow fight rather than a dance, and when it was finished, the pillows insisted on one bout more, like partners who know that they may never meet again. The stories they told, before it was time for Wendy's good-night story! Even Slightly tried to tell a story that night, but the beginning was so fearfully dull that it appalled even himself, and he said gloomily:

'Yes, it is a dull beginning. I say, let us pretend that it is the end.'

And then at last they all got into bed for Wendy's story, the story they loved best, the story Peter hated. Usually when she began to tell this story he left the room or put his hands over his ears; and possibly if he had done either of those things this time they might all still be on the island. But tonight he remained on his stool; and we shall see what happened.

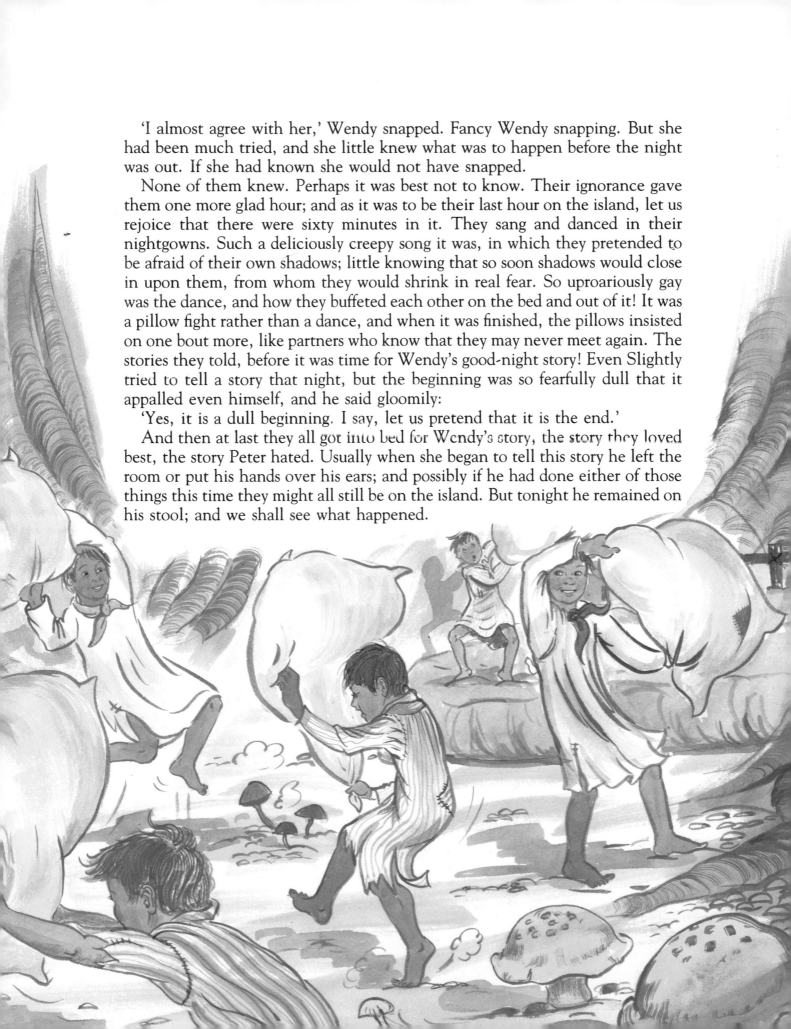

Wendy's Story

*L*ISTEN, THEN,' said Wendy, settling down to her story, with Michael at her feet and seven boys in the bed. 'There was once a gentleman – '

'I had rather he had been a lady,' Curly said.

'I wish he had been a white rat,' said Nibs.

'Quiet,' their mother admonished them. 'There was a lady also, and the gentleman's name was Mr Darling, and her name was Mrs Darling.'

'I knew them,' John said, to annoy the others.

'I think I knew them,' said Michael rather doubtfully.

'They were married, you know,' explained Wendy, 'and what do you think they had?'

'White rats,' cried Nibs, inspired.

'No.'

'It's awfully puzzling,' said Tootles, who knew the story by heart.

'Quiet, Tootles. They had three descendants.'

'What is descendants?'

'Well, you are one, Twin.'

'Do you hear that, John? I am a descendant.'

'Descendants are only children,' said John.

'Oh dear, oh dear,' sighed Wendy. 'Now, these three children had a faithful nurse called Nana; but Mr Darling was angry with her and chained her up in the yard; and so all the children flew away.'

'It's an awfully good story,' said Nibs.

'They flew away,' Wendy continued, 'to the Never Land, where the lost children are.'

'I just thought they did,' Curly broke in excitedly. 'I don't know how it is, but I just thought they did.'

'O Wendy,' cried Tootles, 'was one of the lost children called Tootles?'

'Yes, he was.'

'I am in a story. Hurrah, I am in a story, Nibs!'

'Hush. Now, I want you to consider the feelings of the unhappy parents with all their children flown away.'

'Oo!' they all moaned, though they were not really considering the feelings of the unhappy parents one jot.

'Think of the empty beds!'

'Oo!'

'It's awfully sad,' the first Twin said cheerfully.

'I don't see how it can have a happy ending,' said the second Twin. 'Do you, Nibs?'

'I'm frightfully anxious.'

'If you knew how great is a mother's love,' Wendy told them triumphantly, 'you would have no fear.' She had now come to the part that Peter hated.

'I do like a mother's love,' said Tootles, hitting Nibs with a pillow. 'Do you like a mother's love, Nibs?'

'I do just,' said Nibs, hitting back.

'You see,' Wendy said complacently, 'our heroine knew that the mother would always leave the window open for her children to fly back by; so they stayed away for years and had a lovely time.'

'Did they ever go back?'

'Let us now,' said Wendy, bracing herself for her finest effort, 'take a peep into the future,' and they all gave themselves the twist that makes peeps into the future easier. 'Years have rolled by; and who is this elegant lady alighting at London Station?'

'O Wendy, who is she?' cried Nibs, every bit as excited as if he didn't know.

'Can it be – yes – no – it is – the fair Wendy!'

'Oh!'

'And who are the two noble portly figures accompanying her, now grown to man's estate? Can they be John and Michael? They are!'

That was a story, and they were as pleased with it as the fair narrator herself. So great indeed was their faith in a mother's love that they felt they could afford to be callous for a bit longer.

But there was one who knew better; and when Wendy finished he uttered a hollow groan.

'What is it, Peter?' she cried, running to him, thinking he was ill.

'Wendy, you are wrong about mothers.'

They all gathered round him in fright, so alarming was his agitation; and with a fine candour he told them what he had hitherto concealed.

'Long ago,' he said, 'I thought like you that my mother would always keep the window open for me; so I stayed away for moons and moons and moons, and then flew back; but the window was barred, for mother had forgotten all about me, and there was another little boy sleeping in my bed.'

I am not sure that this was true, but Peter thought it was true; and it scared him.

'Are you sure mothers are like that?'

'Yes.'

So this was the truth about mothers. The toads!

Still it is best to be careful; and no one knows so quickly as a child when he should give in. 'Wendy, let us go home,' cried John and Michael together.

'Yes,' she said, clutching them.

'Not tonight?' asked the lost boys, bewildered.

'At once,' Wendy replied resolutely, for the horrible thought had come to her: 'Perhaps mother is in mourning by this time.'

This dread made her forgetful of what must be Peter's feelings, and she said to him rather sharply, 'Peter, will you make the necessary arrangements?'

'If you wish it,' he replied as coolly as if she had asked him to pass the nuts.

Not so much as a sorry-to-lose-you between them! If she did not mind the parting, he was going to show her, was Peter, that neither did he.

But of course he cared very much; and he was full of wrath against grown-ups, who spoil everything.

While he went to give the necessary instructions to the redskins, an unworthy scene was enacted underground. Panic-stricken at the thought of losing Wendy, the lost boys advanced upon her threateningly.

'It will be worse than before she came,' they cried.

'We shan't let her go.'

'Let's keep her prisoner.'

'Aye, chain her up.'

In her extremity an instinct told her to which of them to turn.

'Tootles,' she cried, 'I appeal to you!'

Was it not strange? She appealed to Tootles, quite the silliest one.

Grandly, however, did Tootles respond. For that one moment he dropped his silliness and spoke with dignity.

'I am just Tootles,' he said, 'and nobody minds me. But the first who does not behave to Wendy like an English gentleman I will blood him severely.'

He drew his sword; and for that instant his sun was at noon.

The others held back uneasily. Then Peter returned, and they saw at once that they would get no support from him. He would keep no girl in the Never Land against her will.

'Wendy,' he said, striding up and down, 'I have asked the redskins to guide you through the wood, as flying tires you so.'

'Thank you, Peter.'

'Then,' he continued in the short sharp voice of one accustomed to be obeyed. 'Tinker Bell will take you across the sea.'

Of course Tink was delighted to hear that Wendy was going; but she was determined not to be her guide. Peter had to speak to her sternly.

In the meantime the boys were gazing very forlornly at Wendy, now equipped with John and Michael for the journey. By this time they were dejected, not merely because they were about to lose her, but also because they felt that she was going off to something nice to which they had not been invited.

Crediting them with a nobler feeling, Wendy melted.

'Dear ones,' she said, 'if you will all come with me I feel almost sure that I can get my father and mother to adopt you.'

The invitation was meant specially for Peter; but each of the boys was thinking exclusively of himself, and at once they jumped with joy.

'But won't they think us rather a handful?' Nibs asked in the middle of his jump.

'Oh, no,' said Wendy, rapidly thinking it out, 'it will only mean having a few beds in the drawing room; they can be hidden behind screens when visitors call.'

'Peter, can we go?' they all cried imploringly.

'All right,' Peter replied with a bitter smile; and immediately they rushed to get their things.

'And now, Peter,' Wendy said, thinking she had put everything right, 'I am going to give you your medicine before you go.' She loved to give them medicine, and undoubtedly gave them too much. Of course it was only water, but she always shook the bottle and counted the drops, which gave it a certain medicinal quality. On this occasion, however, she did not give Peter his medicine, for just as she had prepared it, she saw a look on his face that made her heart sink.

'Get your things, Peter,' she cried, shaking.

'No. I am not going with you, Wendy.'

'Yes, Peter.'

'No.'

To show that her departure would leave him unmoved, he skipped up and down the room, playing gaily on his pipes. She had to run about after him, though it was rather undignified.

'To find your mother,' she coaxed.

'No, no,' he told Wendy decisively; 'perhaps she would say I was old, and I just want to be a little boy and to have fun.'

'But, Peter – '

'No.'

And so the others had to be told.

'Peter isn't coming.'

Peter not coming! They gazed blankly at him, their sticks over their backs and on each stick a bundle. Their first thought was that if Peter was not going he had probably changed his mind about letting them go.

But he was far too proud for that. 'If you find your mothers,' he said darkly, 'I hope you will like them.'

Most of them began to look rather doubtful. After all, their faces said, were they not noodles to want to go?

'Now then,' cried Peter, 'no fuss, no blubbering; good-bye, Wendy'; and he held out his hand cheerily, quite as if they must really go now, for he had something important to do.

She had to take his hand, as there was no indication that he would prefer a thimble.

'You will remember about changing your flannels, Peter?' she said, lingering over him. She was always so particular about their flannels.

'Yes.'

'And you will take your medicine?'

'Yes.'

That seemed to be everything; and an awkward pause followed. Peter, however, was not the kind that breaks down before people. 'Are you ready, Tinker Bell?' he called out.

'Aye, aye,' she tinkled.

'Then lead the way.'

Tink darted up the nearest tree; but no one followed her, for it was at this moment that the pirates made their dreadful attack upon the redskins. Above, where all had been so still, the air was rent with shrieks and the clash of steel. Below, there was dead silence. Mouths opened and remained open. Wendy fell on her knees, but her arms were extended towards Peter. All arms were extended to him, as if suddenly blown in his direction; they were beseeching him mutely not to desert them. As for Peter, he seized his sword, the same he thought he had slain Barbecue with; and the lust of battle was in his eye.

74

The Children Are Carried Off

*T*HE PIRATE attack had been a complete surprise; a sure proof that the unscrupulous Hook had conducted it improperly, for to surprise redskins fairly is beyond the wit of the white man.

By all the unwritten laws of Indian warfare it is always the redskin who attacks, and he does it just before the dawn, at which time he knows the courage of the whites to be at its lowest ebb.

That this was the usual procedure was so well known to Hook that in disregarding it he cannot be excused on the plea of ignorance. No thought of waiting to be attacked appears from first to last to have visited his subtle mind; he would not even hold off till the night was nearly spent; on he pounded with no policy but to fall to.

The Piccaninnies, trusting implicitly in his honour, were confounded by these treacherous tactics. Yet, terrible as the sudden appearance of the pirates must have been to them, they remained stationary for a moment, not a muscle moving; as if the foe had come by invitation. Then they seized their weapons, and the air was torn with their war-cry. But it was now too late.

It is no part of ours to describe what was a massacre rather than a fight. Thus perished many of the flower of the Piccaninny tribe. Not all died unavenged, for with Lean Wolf fell Alf Mason, to disturb the Spanish Main no more; among others who bit the dust were Geo. Scourie, Chas. Turley, and the Alsatian Foggerty. Turley fell to the tomahawk of the terrible Panther, who ultimately cut a way through the pirates with Tiger Lily and a small remnant of the tribe.

To what extent Hook is to blame for his tactics on this occasion is for the historian to decide. Had he waited till the proper hour he and his men would probably have been butchered; in judging him it is only fair to take this into account. What he should perhaps have done was to tell his opponents that he proposed to follow a new method. On the other hand this, by destroying the element of surprise, would have made his strategy of no avail. The whole question is beset with difficulties. One cannot at least withhold a reluctant admiration for the wit that had conceived so bold a scheme, and the fell genius with which it was carried out.

The night's work was not yet over, for it was not the redskins he had come to

destroy; they were but the bees to be smoked, so that he should get at the honey. It was Pan he wanted, Pan and Wendy and their band, but chiefly Pan.

Peter was such a small boy that one wonders at the man's hatred of him. True, he had flung Hook's arm to the crocodile; but even this and the increased insecurity of life to which it led, owing to the crocodile's pertinacity, hardly account for a vindictiveness so relentless and malignant. The truth is that there was something about Peter which goaded the pirate captain to frenzy. It was not his courage, it was not his engaging appearance, it was not – there is no beating about the bush, for we know quite well what it was, and have got to tell. It was Peter's cockiness.

This had got on Hook's nerves; it made his iron claw twitch, and at night it disturbed him like an insect. While Peter lived, the tortured man felt that he was a lion in a cage into which a sparrow had come.

The question now was how to get down the trees, or how to get his men down. He ran his greedy eye over the dogs, searching for the thinnest ones. They wriggled uncomfortably, for they knew that he would not scruple to ram them down with poles.

In the meantime, what of the boys? We have seen them at the first clang of weapons, turned as it were into stone figures, open-mouthed, all appealing with outstretched arms to Peter; and we return to them as their mouths close, and their arms fall to their sides. The pandemonium above has ceased almost as suddenly as it arose, passed like a fierce gust of wind; but they know that in the passing it has determined their fate.

Which side has won?

The pirates, listening eagerly at the mouths of the trees, heard the question put by every boy – and they also heard Peter's answer.

'If the redskins have won,' he said, 'they will beat the tom-tom. It is always their sign of victory.'

77

Now Smee had found the tom-tom, and was at that moment sitting on it. 'You will never hear the tom-tom again,' he muttered, but inaudibly of course, for strict silence had been enjoined. To his amazement Hook signed him to beat the tom-tom; and slowly there came to Smee an understanding of the dreadful wickedness of the order. Never, probably, had this simple man admired Hook so much.

Twice Smee beat upon the instrument, and then stopped to listen gleefully.

'The tom-tom,' the miscreants heard Peter cry; 'an Indian victory!'

The doomed children answered with a cheer that was music to the black hearts above, and almost immediately they repeated their goodbyes to Peter. This puzzled the pirates, but all their other feelings were swallowed by a base delight that the enemy were about to come up the trees. They smirked at each other and rubbed their hands. Rapidly and silently Hook gave his orders: one man to each tree, and the others to arrange themselves in a line two yards apart.

Do You Believe in Fairies?

THE MORE quickly this horror is disposed of the better. The first to emerge from his tree was Curly. He rose out of it into the arms of Cecco, who flung him to Smee, who flung him to Starkey, who flung him to Bill Jukes, who flung him to Noodler, and so he was tossed from one to another till he fell at the feet of the black pirate. All the boys were plucked from their trees in this ruthless manner; and several of them were in the air at a time, like bales of goods flung from hand to hand.

A different treatment was accorded to Wendy, who came last. With ironical politeness Hook raised his hat to her and, offering her his arm, escorted her to the spot where the others were being gagged. He did it with such an air, he was so frightfully distinguished, that she was too fascinated to cry out. She was only a little girl and, for a moment, Hook entranced her.

The boys were tied to prevent their flying away, doubled up with their knees close to their ears; and for the trussing of them the black pirate had cut a rope into nine equal pieces. All went well until Slightly's turn came, when he was found to be like those irritating parcels that use up all the string in going round and leave no ends with which to tie a knot. The pirates kicked him in their rage, just as you would kick the parcel (though in fairness you should kick the string). Strange to say it was Hook who told them to belay their violence. His lip was curled with malicious triumph. While his dogs were merely sweating because every time they tried to pack the unhappy lad tight in one part he bulged out in another, Hook's master mind was probing not for effects but for causes. His exultation showed that he had found them. Slightly, white to the gills, knew that Hook had surprised his secret, which was this:

Slightly had recently grown rather fat and, unknown to the others, he had whittled his tree to make it fit him. The hole, Hook observed, was large enough to fit a man. Peter at last lay at his mercy. But no word of the dark design that now formed in the subterranean caverns of his mind crossed his lips; he merely signed that the captives were to be conveyed to the ship, and that he would be alone.

How to convey them? Hunched up in their ropes they might indeed be rolled downhill like barrels, but most of the way lay through a swamp. Again Hook's genius surmounted difficulties. He indicated that the little house must be used as a conveyance. The children were flung into it, four stout pirates raised it on their shoulders, the others fell in behind, and singing the hateful pirate chorus the strange procession set off through the wood. As the little house disappeared in the forest, a brave though tiny jet of smoke issued from its chimney as if defying Hook.

Hook saw it, and it did Peter a bad service. It dried up any trickle of pity for him that may have remained in the pirate's infuriated breast.

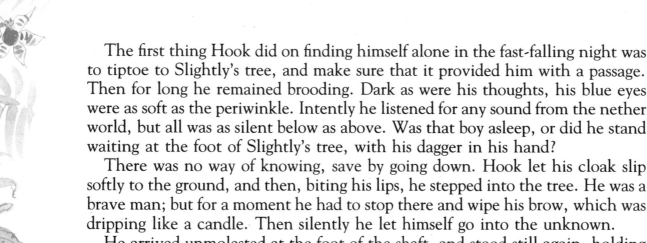

The first thing Hook did on finding himself alone in the fast-falling night was to tiptoe to Slightly's tree, and make sure that it provided him with a passage. Then for long he remained brooding. Dark as were his thoughts, his blue eyes were as soft as the periwinkle. Intently he listened for any sound from the nether world, but all was as silent below as above. Was that boy asleep, or did he stand waiting at the foot of Slightly's tree, with his dagger in his hand?

There was no way of knowing, save by going down. Hook let his cloak slip softly to the ground, and then, biting his lips, he stepped into the tree. He was a brave man; but for a moment he had to stop there and wipe his brow, which was dripping like a candle. Then silently he let himself go into the unknown.

He arrived unmolested at the foot of the shaft, and stood still again, holding his breath, which had almost left him. As his eyes became accustomed to the dim light various objects in the home under the trees took shape; but the only one on which his greedy gaze rested was the great bed. On the bed lay Peter fast asleep.

Unaware of the tragedy being enacted above, Peter had continued, for a little time after the children left, to play gaily on his pipes; no doubt rather a forlorn attempt to prove to himself that he did not care. Then he decided not to take his medicine, so as to grieve Wendy. Then he lay down on the bed outside the coverlet, to vex her still more; for she had always tucked them inside it. Then he nearly cried; but it struck him how indignant she would be if he laughed instead; so he laughed a haughty laugh and fell asleep in the middle of it.

Sometimes, though not often, he had dreams, and they were more painful than the dreams of other boys. For hours he could not be separated from these dreams, though he wailed piteously in them. They had to do, I think, with the riddle of his existence. At such times Wendy used to take him out of bed and sit with him on her lap, soothing him, and when he grew calmer she put him back to bed before he quite woke up, so that he should not know of the indignity to which she had subjected him. But on this occasion he had fallen at once into a dreamless sleep. One arm dropped over the edge of the bed, one leg arched, and the unfinished part of his laugh was stranded on his mouth, which was open, showing the pearly teeth.

Thus defenceless, Hook found him. He stood silent at the foot of the tree looking across the chamber at his enemy. Did no feeling of compassion disturb his sombre breast? The man was not wholly evil; he loved flowers and sweet music (he was himself no mean performer on the harpsichord), and let it be frankly admitted, the idyllic nature of the scene stirred him profoundly. Mastered by his better self, he would have returned reluctantly up the tree, but for one thing.

What stayed him was Peter's impertinent appearance as he slept. The open mouth, the drooping arm, the arched knee: they were such a personification of cockiness as, taken together, will never again, one may hope, be presented to

eyes so sensitive to their offensiveness. They steeled Hook's heart. If his rage had broken him into a hundred pieces, every one of them would have disregarded the incident and leapt at the sleeper.

Though a light from the one lamp shone dimly on the bed, Hook stood in darkness himself, and at the first stealthy step forward he discovered an obstacle, the door of Slightly's tree. It did not entirely fill the opening, and he had been looking over it. Feeling for the catch, he found to his fury that it was low down, beyond his reach. To his disordered brain it seemed then that the irritating quality in Peter's face and figure visibly increased, and he rattled the door and flung himself against it. Was his enemy to escape him after all?

But what was that? The red in his eye had caught sight of Peter's medicine standing on a ledge within easy reach. He guessed what it was straightway, and immediately he knew that the sleeper was in his power.

Lest he should be taken alive, Hook always carried about his person a dreadful drug, blended by himself and boiled down in a yellow liquid quite unknown to science, which was probably the most virulent poison in existence.

Five drops of this he now added to Peter's cup. His hand shook, but it was in exultation rather than in shame. As he did it he avoided glancing at the sleeper, but not lest pity should unnerve him; merely to avoid spilling. Then one long gloating look he cast upon his victim, and turning, wormed his way with difficulty up the tree. As he emerged at the top he looked the very spirit of evil breaking from its hole. Donning his hat at its most rakish angle, he wound his cloak around him, holding one end in front as if to conceal his person from the night, of which it was the blackest part, and muttering strangely to himself stole away through the trees.

Peter slept on. The light guttered and went out, leaving him in darkness; but still he slept. It must have been not less than ten o'clock by the crocodile, when he suddenly sat up in his bed, wakened by he knew not what. It was a soft cautious tapping on the door of his tree.

Peter felt for his dagger till his hand gripped it. Then he spoke. 'Who is that?'

'Let me in, Peter.'

It was Tink, and quickly he unbarred the door. She flew in excitedly, her face flushed and her dress stained with mud.

'What is it?'

'Oh, you could never guess,' she cried, and offered him three guesses.

'Out with it!' he shouted; and in one long ungrammatical sentence she told of the capture of Wendy and the boys.

Peter's heart bobbed up and down as he listened. Wendy bound, and on the pirate ship; she who loved everything to be just so!

'I'll rescue her,' he cried, leaping at his weapons. As he leapt he thought of something he could do to please her. He could take his medicine.

His hand closed on the fatal draught.

'No!' shrieked Tinker Bell, who had heard Hook muttering about his deed as he sped through the forest.

'Why not?'

'It is poisoned.'

'Poisoned? Who could have poisoned it?'

'Hook.'

'Don't be silly. How could Hook have got down here?'

Tinker Bell could not explain this, for even she did not know the dark secret of Slightly's tree. Nevertheless Hook's words had left no room for doubt. The cup was poisoned.

'Besides,' said Peter, quite believing himself, 'I never fell asleep.'

He raised the cup. No time for words now; time for deeds: and with one of her lightning movements Tink got between his lips and the draught, and drained it to the dregs.

'Why, Tink, how dare you drink my medicine?'

But she did not answer. Already she was reeling in the air.

'What is the matter with you?' cried Peter, suddenly afraid.

'It was poisoned, Peter,' she told him softly, 'and now I am going to be dead.'

'O Tink, did you drink it to save me?'

'Yes.'

'But why, Tink?'

Her wings would scarcely carry her now, but in reply she alighted on his shoulder and gave his chin a loving bite. She whispered in his ear, 'You silly ass'; and then, tottering to her chamber, lay down on the bed.

Her voice was so low that Peter could hardly hear what she said. He bent his head closer. She was saying that she thought she could get well again if children believed in fairies.

Peter flung out his arms. There were no children there, and it was night-time. But he addressed all who might be dreaming of the Never Land, and who were therefore nearer to him than you think; boys and girls in their nighties, and naked papooses in their baskets hung from trees.

'Do you believe?' he cried.

Tink sat up in bed almost briskly to listen to her fate.

She fancied she heard faint answers in the affirmative, and then again she wasn't sure.

'What do you think?' she asked Peter.

'If you believe,' he shouted to them, 'clap you hands. Don't let Tink die!'

Many clapped.

Some didn't.

A few little beasts hissed.

The clapping stopped suddenly, as if countless mothers had rushed to their children's bedrooms to see what on earth was happening; but already Tink was saved. First her voice grew strong; then she popped out of bed; then she was flashing through the room more merry and impudent than ever. She never thought of thanking those who believed, but she would have liked to get at the ones who had hissed.

'And now to rescue Wendy.'

The moon was riding in a cloudy heaven when Peter rose from his tree, begirt with weapons, to set out upon his perilous quest. It was not such a night as he would have chosen. He had hoped to fly, keeping not far from the ground so that nothing should escape his eyes; but to have flown low would have meant trailing his shadow through the trees, thus disturbing the birds and acquainting a watchful foe that he was astir.

There was no other course but to press forward in redskin fashion, at which happily he was adept. But in what direction? A slight fall of snow had obliterated all footmarks, and a deathly silence lay over the island, as if for a space Nature stood still in horror of the recent carnage. He had taught the children something of the forest lore that he had learned from Tiger Lily and Tinker Bell, and he knew that in their dire hour they were not likely to forget it. Slightly, if he had an opportunity, would mark the trees, for instance. Curly would drop seeds, and Wendy would leave her handkerchief at some important place. But morning was needed to search for such guidance, and he could not wait.

The crocodile passed him, but not another living thing, not a sound, not a movement; and yet he knew well that sudden death might be at the next tree, or stalking him from behind.

He swore this terrible oath: 'Hook or me this time.'

Now he crawled forward like a snake; and again, erect, he darted across a space on which the moonlight played; one finger on his lips and his dagger at the ready. He was frightfully happy.

The Pirate Ship

NEAR THE mouth of the pirate river, the *Jolly Roger* lay low in the water, a rakish looking craft foul to the hull, every beam in her detestable, the cannibal of the seas. She was wrapped in the blanket of night, through which no sound from her could have reached the shore. There was little sound save the whirr of the ship's sewing machine at which Smee sat, ever industrious and obliging, the essence of the commonplace, pathetic Smee.

A few pirates leant over the bulwarks; others sprawled by barrels over games of dice and cards; and the exhausted four who had carried the little house lay prone on the deck, where even in their sleep they rolled skilfully to this side or that out of Hook's reach, lest he should claw them mechanically in passing.

Hook trod the deck in thought. O man unfathomable. It was his hour of triumph. Peter had been removed for ever from his path, and all the other boys were on the brig, about to walk the plank. It was his grimmest deed since the days when he had brought Barbecue to heel; and knowing as we do how vain a creature is man, could we be surprised had he now paced the deck elatedly, puffed up by the winds of his success?

But there was no elation in his gait, which kept pace with the action of his sombre mind. Hook was profoundly dejected.

He was often thus when communing with himself on board ship in the quietude of the night. It was because he was so terribly alone. This inscrutable man never felt more alone than when surrounded by his dogs. They were socially so inferior to him. For Hook (that was not his true name) was a Public School Man (Eton actually).

As he paced the deck, perspiration dripping down his sallow countenance, there came to him a presentiment of his early dissolution. It was as if Peter's terrible oath had boarded the ship. He felt a gloomy desire to make his dying speech, lest presently there should be no time for it.

'Better for Hook,' he cried, 'if he had less ambition.' It was in his darkest hours only that he referred to himself in the third person.

'No little children love me.'

Strange that he should think of this, which had never troubled him before; perhaps the sewing machine brought it to his mind. For long he muttered to himself, staring at Smee, who, humming placidly at his work, was convinced that all children feared him.

Feared him! Feared Smee! There was not a child on board the brig that night who did not already love him. He had said horrid things to them and hit them with the palm of his hand, because he could not hit them with his fist; but they had only clung to him the more. Michael had tried on his spectacles.

To tell poor Smee that they thought him lovable! Hook itched to do it, but it seemed too brutal. Instead, he revolved this mystery in his mind: why do they find Smee lovable? He perused the problem like the sleuth-hound that he was. If Smee was lovable what was it that made him so? What?

With a cry of rage he raised his iron hand over Smee's head; but he did not tear. Instead, he slumped to the deck. He was completely flummoxed.

His dogs thinking him out the way for a time, discipline instantly relaxed; and they broke into a bacchanalian dance, which brought him to his feet at once; all traces of human weakness gone.

'Quiet, you scugs,' he cried, 'or I'll cast anchor in you': and at once the din was hushed. 'Are all the children chained, so they cannot fly away?'

'Aye, aye.'

'Then hoist them up.'

The wretched prisoners were dragged from the hold, all except Wendy, and ranged in line in front of him. For a time he seemed unconscious of their presence. He lolled at his ease, humming snatches of a rude song and fingering a pack of cards.

'Now then, bullies,' he said briskly, 'six of you walk the plank tonight, but I have room for two cabin boys. Which of you is it to be?'

'Don't irritate him unnecessarily,' had been Wendy's instructions in the hold; so Tootles stepped forward politely.

'You see, sir,' he explained prudently, 'I don't think my mother would like me to be a pirate. Would your mother like you to be a pirate, Slightly?'

'I don't think so,' Slightly said mournfully, as if he wished that things had been otherwise, 'Would your mother like you to be a pirate, Twin?'

'I don't think so,' said the first Twin, as clever as the others. 'Nibs, would – ?'

'Stow this gab,' roared Hook. 'You, boy,' he said, addressing John, 'you look as if you had a little pluck in you. Didst never want to be a pirate, my hearty?'

Now John had sometimes experienced this hankering, and he was struck by Hook's picking him out.

'I once thought of calling myself Red-handed Jack,' he said diffidently.

'And a good name too. We'll call you that here, bully, if you join.'

'What do you think, Michael?' asked John.

'What would you call me if I join?' Michael demanded.

'Blackbeard Joe.'

Michael was naturally impressed. 'What do you think, John?' He wanted John to decide, and John wanted him to decide.

'Shall we still be respectful subjects of the King?' John inquired.

Through Hook's teeth came the answer: 'You would have to swear, "Down with the King."'

Perhaps John had not behaved very well so far, but he shone out now.

'Then I refuse,' he cried, banging the barrel in front of Hook.

'And I refuse,' cried Michael.

'Rule Britannia!' squeaked Curly.

'That seals your doom,' roared Hook. 'Bring up their mother. Get the plank ready.'

They were only boys, and they went white as they saw Jukes and Cecco preparing the fatal plank. But they tried to look brave when Wendy was brought up.

No words of mine can tell you how Wendy despised those pirates. To the boys there was at least some glamour in the pirate calling, but all that she saw was that the ship had not been scrubbed for years. There was not a port-hole on the grimy glass of which you might not have written with your finger, 'Dirty pig', and she had already written it on several. But as the boys gathered round her she had no thought, of course, save for them.

'So, my beauty,' said Hook, as if he spoke in syrup, 'you are to see your children walk the plank.'

'Are they to die?' asked Wendy, with a look of such frightful contempt that he nearly fainted.

'They are,' he snarled. 'Silence all,' he called gloatingly, 'for a mother's last words to her children.'

At this moment Wendy was grand. 'These are my last words, dear boys,' she said firmly. 'I feel that I have a message to you from your real mothers, and it is this: "We hope our sons will die like English gentlemen."'

Even the pirates were awed; and Tootles cried out hysterically, 'I am going to do what my mother hopes. What are you to do, Nibs?'

'What my mother hopes. What are you to do, Twin?'

'What my mother hopes. John, what are – ?'

But Hook had found his voice again.

'Tie her up,' he shouted.

It was Smee who tied her to the mast. 'See here, honey,' he whispered, 'I'll save you if you promise to be my mother.'

But not even for Smee would she make such a promise. 'I would almost rather have no children at all,' she said disdainfully.

It was sad to know that not one boy was looking at her as Smee tied her to the mast; the eyes of all were on the plank; that last little walk they were about to take. They were no longer able to hope that they would walk it manfully, for the capacity to think had gone from them; they could stare and shiver only.

Hook smiled on them with his teeth closed, and took a step towards Wendy. His intention was to turn her face so that she should see the boys walking the plank one by one. But he never reached her, he never heard the cry of anguish he hoped to wring from her. He heard something else instead.

It was the terrible tick-tick of the crocodile.

They all heard it – pirates, boys, Wendy; and immediately every head was blown in one direction; not to the water whence the sound had proceeded, but towards Hook. All knew that what was about to happen concerned him alone, and that from being actors they were suddenly become spectators.

Very frightful it was to see the change that came over him. It was as if he had been clipped at every joint. He fell in a little heap.

The sound came steadily nearer; and in advance of it came this ghastly thought, 'The crocodile is about to board the ship.'

Even the iron claw hung inactive; as if knowing that it was not on the menu. Left so fearfully alone, any other man would have lain with his eyes shut where he fell; but the gigantic brain of Hook was still working, and under its guidance he crawled on his knees along the deck as far from the sound as he could go. It was only when he was brought up against the bulwarks that he spoke.

'Hide me,' he cried hoarsely.

They gathered round him; all eyes averted from the thing that was coming aboard. They had no thought of fighting. It was Fate.

Only when Hook was hidden from them did curiosity loosen the limbs of the boys so that they could rush to the ship's side to see the crocodile climbing it. Then they got the strangest surprise of this Night of Nights; for it was no crocodile that was coming to their aid. It was Peter.

He signed to them not to give a cry that might arouse suspicion. Then he went on ticking.

`Hook or Me!´

WHEN PETER had seen the crocodile pass by, it had not been ticking. He concluded rightly that the clock had run down and at once considered how he could turn the catastrophe to his own use. He decided to tick, so that wild beasts should believe he was the crocodile and let him pass unmolested. He ticked superbly, but with one unforeseen result. The crocodile was among those who heard the sound, and it followed him, though whether with the purpose of regaining what it had lost, or merely as a friend under the belief that it was again ticking itself will never be certainly known, for, like all slaves to a fixed idea, it was a stupid beast.

Peter reached the shore and swam towards the pirate ship with but one thought: 'Hook or me this time.' He had ticked so long that he now went on ticking without knowing that he was doing it. He was amazed to see the pirates cowering from him, with Hook in their midst as abject as if he had heard the crocodile.

The crocodile! No sooner did Peter remember it than he heard the ticking. At first he thought the sound did come from the crocodile, then he realized that he was doing it himself. 'How clever of me,' he thought at once, and signed to the boys not to burst into applause.

It was at this moment that Ed Teynte the quartermaster emerged from the fo'c'sle and came along the deck. Peter struck true and deep. John clapped his hands on the ill-fated pirate's mouth to stifle the dying groan. He fell forward. Four boys caught him to prevent the thud. Peter gave the signal, and the carrion was cast overboard. There was a splash, and then silence.

'One!' (Slightly had begun to count.)

Peter, every inch of him on tiptoe, vanished into the cabin, just as the pirates emerged from their hiding places.

'It's gone, captain,' Smee said, wiping his spectacles. 'All's still again.'

Hook listened so intently that he could have caught the echo of the tick. There was not a sound, and he drew himself up firmly to his full height.

'Then here's to Johnny Plank,' he cried brazenly, hating the boys more than ever because they had seen him unbend. He broke into the villainous ditty:

> 'Yo ho, yo ho, the frisky plank,
> You walks along it so,
> Till it goes down and you goes down
> To Davy Jones below!'

To terrorize the prisoners the more, though with a certain loss of dignity, he danced along an imaginary plank, grimacing at them as he sang; and when he finished he cried, 'Do you want a touch of the cat before you walk the plank?'

At that they fell on their knees. 'No, no,' they cried so piteously that every pirate smiled.

'Fetch the cat, Jukes,' said Hook; 'it's in the cabin.'

The cabin! Peter was in the cabin! The children gazed at each other.

'Aye, aye,' said Jukes blithely, and he strode into the cabin. They followed him with their eyes; they scarce knew that Hook had resumed his song, his dogs joining in with him:

> 'Yo ho, yo ho, the scratching cat,
> Its tails are nine, you know,
> And when they're writ upon your back – '

What was the last line will never be known, for of a sudden the song was stayed by a dreadful screech from the cabin. It wailed through the ship, and died away. Then was heard a crowing sound which was well understood by the boys, but to the pirates was almost more eerie than the screech.

'What was that?' cried Hook.

'Two,' said Slightly solemnly.

The Italian Cecco hesitated for a moment and then swung into the cabin. He tottered out, haggard.

'What's the matter with Bill Jukes, you dog?' hissed Hook, towering over him.

'The matter wi' him is he's dead, stabbed,' replied Cecco in a hollow voice.

'Bill Jukes dead!' cried the startled pirates.

'The cabin's as black as a pit,' Cecco said, almost gibbering, 'but there is something terrible in there: the thing you heard crowing.'

The exultation of the boys, the lowering looks of the pirates, both were seen by Hook.

'Cecco,' he said in his most steely voice, 'go back and fetch me out that doodle-doo.'

Cecco, bravest of the brave, cowered before his captain, crying, 'No, no': but Hook was purring to his claw.

'Did you say you would go, Cecco?' he said musingly.

Cecco went, first flinging up his arms despairingly. There was no more singing, all listened now; and again came a death-screech and again a crow.

No one spoke except Slightly. 'Three,' he said.

Hook rallied his dogs with a gesture. 'Sdeath and odds fish,' he thundered, 'who is to bring me that doodle-doo? I think I heard you volunteer, Starkey.'

'No, by thunder!' Starkey cried, 'I'll swing before I go in there,' and he had the support of the crew.

'Is it mutiny?' asked Hook more pleasantly than ever. 'Starkey's ring-leader.'

'Captain, mercy,' Starkey whimpered, all of a tremble now.

'Shake hands, Starkey,' said Hook, proffering his claw.

Starkey looked round for help, but all deserted him. As he backed Hook advanced, and now the red spark was in his eye. With a despairing scream the pirate leapt into the sea.

'Four,' said Slightly.

'And now,' Hook asked courteously, 'did any other gentleman say mutiny?'

Seizing a lantern, and raising his claw with a menacing gesture, 'I'll bring out that doodle-do myself,' he said, and sped into the cabin.

'Five.' How Slightly longed to say it. He wetted his lips to be ready, but Hook came staggering out, without his lantern.

'Something blew out the light,' he said a little unsteadily.

'Something!' echoed Mullins.

'What of Cecco?' demanded Noodler.

'He's as dead as Jukes,' said Hook shortly.

His reluctance to return to the cabin impressed them all unfavourably, and the mutinous sounds broke forth. Hook had well-nigh forgotten his prisoners, but as he swung round on them now his face lit up again.

'Lads,' he cried to his crew, 'here's a notion. Open the cabin door and drive them in. Let them fight the doodle-doo for their lives. If they kill him, we're so much the better; if he kills them we're none the worse.'

For the last time his dogs admired Hook, and devotedly they did his bidding. The boys, pretending to struggle, were pushed into the cabin and the door was closed on them.

In the cabin Peter had found the thing for which he had gone in search: the key that would free the children of their manacles; and now they all stole forth, armed with such weapons as they could find. First signing them to hide, Peter cut Wendy's bonds, and then nothing could have been easier for them all to fly off together; but one thing barred the way, an oath, 'Hook or me this time.' So when he had freed Wendy, he whispered to her to conceal herself with the others and himself took her place by the mast, her cloak around him so that he should pass for her. Then he took a great breath and crowed.

To the pirates it was a voice crying that all the boys lay slain in the cabin; and they were panic-stricken. Hook tried to hearten them; but like the dogs he had made them they showed him their fangs, and he knew that if he took his eyes off them now they would leap at him.

'Lads,' he said, ready to cajole or strike as need be, but never quailing for an instant, 'I've thought it out. There's a Jonah aboard.'

'Aye,' they snarled, 'a man wi' a hook.'

'No, lads, no, it's the girl. Never was luck on a pirate ship with a woman on board. We'll right the ship when she's gone.'

Some of them remembered that this had been a saying of Flint's. 'It's worth trying,' they said doubtfully.

'Fling the girl overboard,' cried Hook; and they made a rush at the figure in the cloak.

'There's none can save you now, missy,' Mullins hissed jeeringly.

'There's one,' replied the figure.

'Who's that?'

'Peter Pan the avenger!' came the terrible answer; and as he spoke Peter flung off his cloak. Then they all knew who it was that had been undoing them in the cabin, and twice Hook essayed to speak and twice he failed. In that frightful moment I think his fierce heart broke.

At last he cried, 'Cleave him to the brisket,' but without conviction.

'Down, boys, and at them,' Peter's voice rang out; and in another moment the clash of arms was resounding through the ship. Had the pirates kept together it is certain that they would have won; but the onset came when they were all unstrung, and they ran hither and thither, striking wildly, each thinking himself the last survivor of the crew. Man to man they were stronger; but they fought on the defensive only, which enabled the boys to hunt in pairs and choose their quarry. There was little sound to be heard but the clang of weapons, an occasional screech or splash, and Slightly monotonously – five – six – seven – eight – nine – ten – eleven.

I think all were gone when a group of savage boys surrounded Hook, who seemed to have a charmed life, as he kept them at bay in that circle of fire. They had done for his dogs, but this man alone seemed to be a match for them all. Again and again they closed upon him, and again and again he hewed a clear space. He had lifted up one boy with his hook, and was using him as a shield, when another, who just passed his sword through Mullins, sprang into the fray.

'Put up your swords, boys,' cried the newcomer, 'this man is mine.'

Thus suddenly Hook found himself face to face with Peter. The others drew back and formed a ring round them.

For long the two enemies looked at one another; Hook shuddering slightly, and Peter with the strange smile upon his face.

'So, Pan,' said Hook at last, 'this is all your doing.'

'Aye, James Hook,' came the stern answer, 'it is all my doing.'

'Proud and insolent youth,' said Hook, 'prepare to meet thy doom.'

'Dark and sinister man,' Peter answered, 'have at thee.'

Without more words they fell to, and for a space there was no advantage to either blade. Peter was a superb swordsman, and parried with dazzling rapidity. Hook, scarcely his inferior in brilliancy, but not quite so nimble in wrist play, forced him back by the weight of his onset, hoping suddenly to end all with a favourite thrust, taught him long ago by Barbecue at Rio; but to his astonishment he found this thrust turned aside again and again. Then he sought to close and give the quietus with his iron hook, which all this time had been pawing the air; but Peter doubled under it and, lunging fiercely, pierced him in the ribs. At sight of his own blood, whose peculiar colour, you remember, was offensive to him, the sword fell from Hook's hand, and he was at Peter's mercy.

'Now!' cried all the boys; but with a magnificent gesture Peter invited his opponent to pick up his sword. Hook did so instantly.

'To't again,' he cried despairingly.

He fought now like a human flail, and every sweep of that terrible sword would have severed in twain any man or boy who obstructed it; but Peter fluttered round him as if the very wind it made blew him out of the danger zone. And again and again he darted in and pricked.

Hook was now without hope. Abandoning the fight he rushed into the powder magazine and fired it.

'In two minutes,' he cried, 'the ship will be blown to pieces.'

But Peter issued from the powder magazine with the shell in his hands, and calmly flung it overboard.

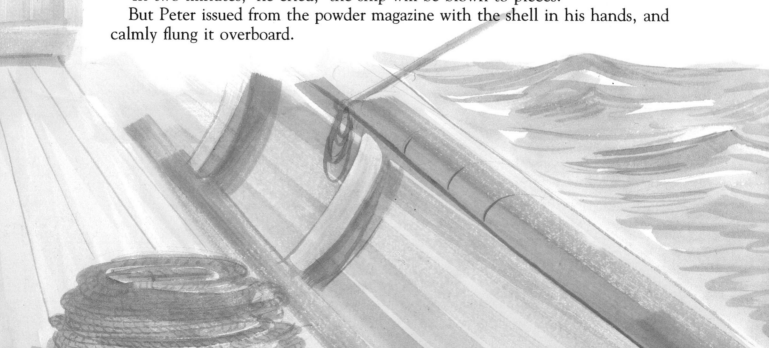

And now, James Hook, thou not wholly unheroic figure, farewell.

For we have come to his last moment.

Seeing Peter slowly advancing upon him through the air with dagger poised, he sprang upon the bulwarks and cast himself into the sea.

He did not know that the crocodile was waiting for him; for we purposely stopped the clock that this knowledge might be spared him: a little mark of respect from us at the end.

Thus perished James Hook. 'Seventeen,' Slightly sang out; but he was not quite correct in his figures. Fifteen paid the penalty for their crimes that night; but two reached the shore; Starkey to be captured by the redskins, who made him nurse for all their papooses, a melancholy come-down for a pirate, and Smee, who henceforth wandered about the world in his spectacles, making a precarious living by saying he was the only man that James Hook had feared.

Wendy, of course, had stood by taking no part in the fight, though watching Peter with glistening eyes; but now that all was over she became prominent again. For the lateness of the hour was almost the biggest thing of all. She got the boys to bed in the pirates' bunks pretty quickly, you may be sure; all but Peter, who strutted up and down on deck, until at last he fell asleep by the side of Long Tom.

The Return Home

BY TWO BELLS that morning they were all stirring their stumps; for there was a big sea running; and Tootles, the bo'sun, was among them with a rope's end in his hand and chewing tobacco. They all donned pirate clothes cut off at the knee, shaved smartly, and tumbled up, with the true nautical roll and hitching their trousers.

It need not be said who was the captain. Nibs and John were first and second mate. There was a woman aboard. The rest were tars before the mast, and lived in the fo'c'sle. Peter had already lashed himself to the wheel; but he piped all hands and delivered a short address to them; said he hoped that they would do their duty like gallant hearties, but that he knew they were the scum of Rio and the Gold Coast, and if they snapped at him he would tear them. His bluff strident words struck the note sailors understand, and they cheered him lustily. Then a few sharp orders were given, and they turned the ship round and nosed her for the mainland.

Captain Pan calculated, after consulting the ship's chart, that if this weather lasted they should strike the Azores about the 21st of June, after which it would save time to fly.

Some of them wanted it to be an honest ship and others were in favour of keeping it a pirate; but the captain treated them as dogs, and they dared not express their wishes to him even in a round robin. Instant obedience was the only safe thing. The general feeling was that Peter was honest just now to lull Wendy's suspicions, but that there might be a change when the new suit was ready, which, against her will, she was making for him out of some of Hook's wickedest garments. It was afterwards whispered among them that on the first night he wore this suit he sat long in the cabin with Hook's cigar-holder in his mouth and one hand clenched, all but the forefinger, which he bent and held threateningly aloft like a hook.

Instead of watching the ship, however, we must now return to that desolate home from which three of our characters had taken heartless flight so long ago.

When the children flew away, Mr Darling felt in his bones that all the blame was his for having chained Nana up, and that from first to last she had been wiser than he. Of course, as we have seen, he was quite a simple man; but he had also a noble sense of justice and a lion courage to do what seemed right to him; and having thought the matter out with anxious care after the flight of the children, he went down on all fours and crawled into Nana's kennel. To all Mrs

Darling's invitations to him to come out he replied sadly but firmly:

'No, my own one, this is the place for me.'

In the bitterness of his remorse he swore that he would never leave the kennel until his children came back. Of course this was a pity; but whatever Mr Darling did he had to do in excess; otherwise he soon gave up doing it. And there never was a more humble man than the proud George Darling, as he sat in the kennel of an evening talking with his wife of their children and all their pretty ways.

Very touching was his deference to Nana, he followed her wishes always.

On that eventful Thursday Mrs Darling was in the children's bedroom, a very sad-eyed woman. Her husband, feeling drowsy, was curled up in the kennel.

'Won't you play me to sleep,' he asked, 'on the piano?' and as she was crossing to the next room he added thoughtlessly, 'And shut that window. I feel a draught.'

'O George, never ask me to do that. The window must always be left open for them, always, always.'

He humbly begged her pardon, and she went and played, and soon he was asleep; and while he slept, Wendy and John and Michael flew into the room.

Oh no. We have written it so, because that was the charming arrangement planned by them when they left the ship; but something must have happened since then, for it is not they who have flown in, it is Peter and Tinker Bell.

Peter's first words tell all.

'Quick, Tink,' he whispered, 'close the window; bar it. That's right. Now you and I must get away by the door; and when Wendy comes she will think her mother has barred her out; and she will have to go back with me.'

Instead of feeling that he was behaving badly, he danced with glee; then he peeped into the next room to see who was playing. He whispered to Tink, 'It's Wendy's mother. She is a pretty lady, but not so pretty as my mother.'

Of course he knew nothing whatever about his mother; but he sometimes bragged about her.

He did not know the tune, which was 'Home, Sweet Home', but he knew it was saying, 'Come back, Wendy, Wendy, Wendy'; and he cried exultantly, 'You will never see Wendy again, lady, for the window is barred.'

He peeped in again to see why the music had stopped; and now he saw that Mrs Darling had laid her head on the piano, and that two tears were sitting on her eyes.

'She wants me to unbar the window,' thought Peter, 'but I won't, not I.'

He peeped again, and the tears were still there, or another two had taken their place.

'She's awfully fond of Wendy,' he said to himself. He was angry with her now for not seeing why she could not have Wendy.

The reason was so simple: 'I'm fond of her too. We can't both have her, lady.'

But the lady would not make the best of it, and he was unhappy. He ceased to look at her, but even then she would not let go of him. He skipped about and made funny faces, but when he stopped it was just as if she were inside him, knocking.

'Oh, all right,' he said at last, and gulped. Then he unbarred the window. 'Come on, Tink,' he cried, with a frightful sneer at the laws of nature; 'we don't want any silly mothers'; and he flew away.

Thus Wendy and John and Michael found the window open for them after all, which of course was more than they deserved. They alighted on the floor, quite unashamed of themselves; and the youngest one had already forgotten his home.

'John,' he said, looking around him, 'I think I have been here before.'

'Of course you have, you silly. There is your old bed.'

'So it is,' Michael said, but not with much conviction.

'I say,' cried John, 'the kennel!' and he dashed across to look inside it.

'Perhaps Nana is inside it,' Wendy said.

But John whistled. 'Hallo,' he said, 'there's a man inside it.'

'It's father!' exclaimed Wendy.

'Let me see father,' Michael begged eagerly, and he took a good look. 'He is not so big as the pirate I killed.'

'Surely,' said John, like one who has lost faith in his memory, 'he used not to sleep in the kennel?'

'John,' Wendy said falteringly, 'perhaps we don't remember the old life as well as we thought we did.' A chill fell upon them.

'It is very careless of mother,' said that young scoundrel John, 'not to be here when we come back.'

It was then that Mrs Darling began playing again.

'It's mother!' cried Wendy, peeping.

'Then you are not really our mother, Wendy?' asked Michael.

'Oh dear!' exclaimed Wendy, with her first real twinge of remorse, 'it is quite time we came back. Let us all slip into our beds, and be there when she comes in, just as if we had never been away.'

And so, when Mrs Darling went back to the children's bedroom to see if her husband was asleep, all the beds were occupied. The children waited for her cry of joy, but it did not come. She saw them but she did not believe they were there. You see, she saw them in their beds so often in her dreams that she thought this was just the dream hanging around her still. She sat down in the chair by the fire.

They could not understand this, and a cold fear fell upon them.

'Mother!' Wendy cried.

'That's Wendy,' she said, but still she was sure it was the dream.

'Mother!'

'That's John,' she said.

'Mother!' cried Michael. He knew her now.

'That's Michael,' she said, and she stretched out her arms for the three little selfish children they would never envelop again. Yes, they did, they went round Wendy and John and Michael, who had slipped out of bed and run to her.

'George, George,' she cried when she could speak; and Mr Darling woke to share her bliss, and Nana came rushing in. There could not have been a lovelier sight; but there was none to see it except a strange boy who was staring in at the window. He had ecstasies innumerable that other children can never know; but he was looking through the window at the one joy from which he must be for ever barred.

When Wendy Grew Up

I HOPE YOU want to know what became of the other boys. They were waiting below to give Wendy time to explain about them; and when they had counted five hundred they went up. They went up by the stair, because they thought this would make a better impression. They stood in a row in front of Mrs Darling, with their hats off, and wishing they were not wearing their pirate clothes. They said nothing, but their eyes asked her to have them.

Of course Mrs Darling said at once that she would have them, and Mr Darling said he would find space for them all in the drawing-room if they fitted in.

As for Peter, he saw Wendy once again before he flew away. He did not exactly come to the window, but he brushed against it in passing, so that she could open it if she liked and call to him. That was what she did.

'Hallo, Wendy, goodbye,' he said.

'Oh dear, are you going away?'

'Yes.'

'You don't feel, Peter,' she said falteringly, 'that you would like to say anything to my parents about a very sweet subject?'

'No.'

'About me, Peter?'

'No.'

Mrs Darling came to the window, for at present she was keeping a sharp eye on Wendy. She told Peter that she had adopted all the other boys, and would like to adopt him also.

'Would you send me to school?' he inquired craftily.

'Yes.'

'I don't want to go to school and learn solemn things,' he told her passionately. 'I don't want to be a man. O Wendy's mother, if I was to wake up and feel there was a beard!'

117

'Peter!' said Wendy the comforter, 'I should love you in a beard'; and Mrs Darling stretched out her arms to him, but he repulsed her.

'Keep back, lady, no one is going to catch me and make me a man.'

'But where are you going to live?'

'With Tink in the house we built for Wendy. The fairies are to put it high up among the tree-tops where they sleep at nights.'

'How lovely,' cried Wendy so longingly that Mrs Darling tightened her grip.

'I shall have such fun,' said Peter, with one eye on Wendy.

'It will be rather lonely in the evening,' she said, 'sitting by the fire.'

'Well then, come with me to the little house.'

'May I, Mummy?'

'Certainly not. I have got you home again, and I mean to keep you.'

'But he does so need a mother.'

'So do you, my love.'

'Oh, all right,' Peter said, as if he had asked her from politeness merely; but Mrs Darling saw his mouth twitch, and she made this handsome offer: to let Wendy go to him for a week every year to do his spring cleaning. Wendy would have preferred a more permanent arrangement; and it seemed to her that spring would be long in coming; but this promise sent Peter away quite gay again. He had no sense of time, and was so full of adventures that all I have told you about him is only a pennyworth of them. I suppose it was because Wendy knew this that her last words to him were these rather plaintive ones:

'You won't forget me, Peter, will you, before spring-cleaning time comes?'

Of course Peter promised; and then he flew away.

All the boys went to school, and they soon saw what goats they had been not to remain on the island; but it was too late now, and soon they settled down to being as ordinary as you or me. It is sad to have to say that the power to fly gradually left them. Want of practice, they called it; but what it really meant was that they no longer believed.

Michael believed longer than the other boys, though they jeered at him; so he was with Wendy when Peter came for her at the end of the first year. She flew away with Peter in the frock she had woven from leaves and berries in the Never Land, and her one fear was that he might notice how short it had become; but he never noticed, he had so much to say about himself.

She had looked forward to thrilling talks with him about old times, but new adventures had crowded the old ones from his mind. He couldn't even remember Captain Hook. But he was exactly as fascinating as ever, and they had a lovely spring cleaning in the little house in the tree-tops.

Next year he did not come to her. She waited in a new frock because the old one simply would not fit; but he never came.

'Perhaps he is ill,' Michael said.

'You know he is never ill.'

Michael came close to her and whispered, with a shiver. 'Perhaps there is no such person, Wendy!' and then Wendy would have cried if Michael had not been crying.

Peter came next spring cleaning; and the strange thing was that he never knew he had missed a year.

119

That was the last time the girl Wendy ever saw him. For a little longer she tried for his sake not to have growing pains; and she felt she was untrue to him when she got a prize for general knowledge. But the years came and went without bringing the careless boy; and when they met again Wendy was a married woman, and Peter was no more to her than a little dust in the box in which she kept her toys. Wendy was grown up. You need not be sorry for her. She was of the kind that likes to grow up. In the end she grew up of her own free will a day quicker than other girls.

All the boys were grown up and done for by this time; so it is scarcely worth while saying anything more about them. You may see the Twins and Nibs and Curly any day going to an office, each carrying a little bag and an umbrella. Michael is an engine-driver. Slightly married a lady of title, and so he became a lord. You see that judge in a wig coming out at the iron door? That used to be Tootles. The bearded man who doesn't know any story to tell his children was once John.

Wendy was married in white with a pink sash. It is strange to think that Peter did not alight in the church and forbid the wedding.

Years rolled on again, and Wendy had a daughter, who was called Jane. She always had an odd inquiring look, and when she was old enough to ask questions they were mostly about Peter Pan. She loved to hear of Peter, and Wendy told her all she could remember in the very nursery from which the famous flight had taken place. It is Jane's nursery now, for her father bought the house from Wendy's father.

They are now embarked on the great adventure of the night when Peter flew in looking for his shadow.

'The foolish fellow,' says Wendy, 'tried to stick it on with soap, and when he could not he cried, and that woke me, and I sewed it on for him.'

'You have missed a bit,' interrupts Jane, who now knows the story better than her mother. 'When you saw him sitting on the floor crying, what did you say?'

'I sat up in bed and I said, "Boy, why are you crying?"'

'Yes, that was it,' says Jane, with a big breath.

'And then he taught us how to fly.'

'Why can't you fly now, mother?'

'Because I am grown up, dearest. When people grow up they forget the way.'

'Why do they forget the way?'

'Because they are no longer gay and innocent and heartless. It is only the gay and innocent and heartless who can fly.'

'What is gay and innocent and heartless? I do wish I was gay and innocent and heartless.'

The story continues. 'We all flew away to the Never Land and the fairies and the pirates and the redskins and the Mermaids' Lagoon, and the home under the ground, and the little house.'

'Yes! Which did you like best of all?'

'I think I liked the home under the ground best of all.'

'Yes, so do I. What was the last thing Peter ever said to you?'

'The last thing he ever said to me was, "Just always be waiting for me, and then some night you will hear me crowing."'

'Yes.'

'But, alas! he forgot all about me.' Wendy said it with a smile. She was as grown up as that.

'What did his crow sound like?' Jane asked one evening.

'It was like this,' Wendy said, trying to imitate Peter's crow.

'No, it wasn't,' Jane said gravely, 'it was like this'; and she did it ever so much better than her mother.

Wendy was a little startled. 'My darling, how can you know?'

'I often hear it when I am sleeping,' said Jane.

'Ah yes, many girls hear it when they are sleeping, but I was the only one who heard it awake.'

'Lucky you,' said Jane.

And then one night came the tragedy. It was the spring of the year, and the story had been told for the night, and Jane was now asleep in her bed. Wendy was sitting on the floor, very close to the fire, so as to see to darn, for there was no other light in the room; and while she sat darning she heard a crow. Then the window blew open as of old, and Peter dropped on the floor.

He was exactly the same as ever, and Wendy saw at once that he still had all his first teeth.

He was a little boy, and she was grown up. She huddled by the fire, not daring to move, helpless and guilty, a big woman.

'Hallo, Wendy,' he said, not noticing any difference, for he was thinking chiefly of himself.

'Hallo, Peter,' she replied faintly, squeezing herself as small as possible. Something inside her was crying, 'Woman, woman, let go of me.'

'Hallo, where is John?' he asked, seeing only one bed occupied.

'John is not here now,' she gasped.

'Is Michael asleep?' he asked, with a careless glance at Jane.

'That is not Michael,' she said.

Now surely he would understand; but not a bit of it.

'Peter,' she said, faltering, 'are you expecting me to fly away with you?'

'Of course, that is why I have come.' He added a little sternly, 'Have you forgotten that this is spring-cleaning time?'

She knew it was useless to say that he had let many spring-cleaning times pass.

'I can't come,' she said apologetically, 'I have forgotten how to fly.'

'I'll soon teach you again.'

'O Peter, don't waste the fairy dust on me.'

She had risen; and now at last a fear assailed him. 'What is it?' he cried, shrinking.

Then she turned up the light, and Peter saw. He gave a cry of pain. 'What is it?' he cried again.

She had to tell him.

'I am old, Peter. I grew up long ago.'

'You promised not to!'

'I couldn't help it. I am a married woman, Peter, and the little girl in the bed is my baby.'

He took a step towards the sleeping child with his dagger upraised. Of course he did not strike. He sat on the floor instead and sobbed; and Wendy did not know how to comfort him, though she could have done it so easily once. She was only a woman now, and she ran out of the room to try to think.

Peter continued to cry, and soon his sobs woke Jane. She sat up in bed and was interested at once.

'Boy,' she said, 'why are you crying?'

Peter rose and bowed to her, and she bowed to him from the bed.

'Hallo,' he said.

'Hallo,' said Jane.

'My name is Peter Pan,' he told her.

'Yes, I know.'

'I came back for my mother,' he explained, 'to take her to the Never Land.'

'Yes, I know,' Jane said, 'I've been waiting for you.'

123

When Wendy returned diffidently she found Peter sitting on the bedpost crowing gloriously, while Jane in her nighty was flying round the room in solemn ecstacy.

'She is my mother,' Peter explained; and Jane descended and stood by his side, with the look on her face that he liked to see on ladies when they gazed at him.

'He does so need a mother,' Jane said.

'Yes, I know,' Wendy admitted rather forlornly; 'no one knows it so well as I.'

'Goodbye,' said Peter to Wendy; and he rose in the air, and the shameless Jane rose with him; it was already her easiest way of moving about.

Wendy rushed to the window.

'No, no,' she cried.

'It is just for spring-cleaning time,' Jane said; 'he wants me always to do his spring cleaning.'

Of course in the end Wendy let them fly away together. Our last glimpse of her shows her at the window, watching them receding into the sky until they were as small as stars.

As you look at Wendy you may see her hair becoming white, and her figure little again, for all this happened long ago. Jane is now a common grown-up with a daughter called Margaret; and every spring-cleaning time, except when he forgets, Peter comes for Margaret and takes her to the Never Land, where she tells him stories about himself, to which he listens eagerly. When Margaret grows up she will have a daughter, who is to be Peter's mother in turn; and thus it will go on, so long as children are gay and innocent and heartless.